BOLD AND BLUE

IN DOG TOWN

SANDY RIDEOUT

ELLEN RIGGS

FREE PREQUEL

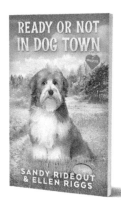

A Rescue Dog and an Unexpected Date with Destiny

Meet Isla McInnis, a reporter who flies across the country to Dorset Hills on a hunch that a sweet little rescue dog named Rio will change her life forever. A quirky band of rescue rebels shows her the true reason she was called to this quaint town in the first place.

Join Sandy Rideout's author newsletter at **Sandyrideout.com** to get the FREE PREQUEL to the Dog Town cozy-romance series at sandyrideout.com.

Bold and Blue in Dog Town

Copyright © 2019 Sandy Rideout

ISBN 978-1-989303-41-2 eBook
ISBN 978-1-989303-40-5 Book
ASIN B081MTTJHC Kindle
ASIN 1989303404 Paperback

Publisher: Sandy Rideout
www.sandyrideout.com
Cover designer: Lou Harper
Editor: Serena Clarke
2103111100

WELCOME TO DOG TOWN!

Dear Reader,

I used to be a diehard cat lady. Then I got my first dog ever and I was a goner! A journalist by training, I interviewed every expert I could find: trainers, breeders, groomers, walkers and more. The journey ultimately brought me here, to Dog Town.

Dorset Hills, better known as *Dog Town*, is famous for being the most dog-friendly place in the world. People come from near and far to enjoy its beautiful landscape and unique charms. Naturally, when so many dogs and dog-lovers unite in one town, mischief and mayhem ensue.

In the Dog Town cozy-romance series, you can expect the humor, the quirky, loveable characters and the edge-of-your-seat suspense that are part of any cozy mystery, but there's a little more romance and a lot less murder. In fact, *no one dies*! I can guarantee you'll laugh out loud and enjoy hair-raising adventures, heartwarming holidays and happily-ever-afters for both humans and pets.

You can read the books in any order, but it's more fun to work your way through the seasons in Dog Town:

- *Ready or Not in Dog Town* (The Beginning)
- *Bitter and Sweet in Dog Town* (Labor Day)
- *A Match Made in Dog Town* (Thanksgiving)

- *Lost and Found in Dog Town* (Christmas)
- *Calm and Bright in Dog Town* (Christmas)
- *Tried and True in Dog Town* (New Year's)
- *Yours and Mine in Dog Town* (Valentine's Day)
- *Nine Lives in Dog Town* (Easter)
- *Great and Small in Dog Town* (Memorial Day)
- *Bold and Blue in Dog Town* (Independence Day)
- *Better or Worse in Dog Town* (Labor Day)

If you fancy more murder with your mystery, be sure to join my newsletter at **Sandyrideout.com** to get the FREE PREQUEL to the Bought-the-Farm Cozy Mystery series. My newsletter is filled with funny stories and photos of my adorable dogs. Don't miss out!

Take care,
Sandy (and Ellen)

CHAPTER ONE

Dorset Hills lost much of its legendary charm at sundown. Everything that made it delightful and unique by day simply switched off at dusk. The dog-themed shops closed. The tasteful gardens and displays faded to grey. And the streets and lakeside promenade lost their constant parades of dogs, which were, after all, the main attraction for the city known as the best place in all of North America for dogs and dog lovers.

The other main attraction, at least according to City Council, was the collection of massive bronze statues fashioned after various purebred dogs. After nightfall, these eight-foot creatures became monstrous. Parents complained of needing to map their evening travels to avoid terrifying their children near bedtime. This had become complicated now that nearly every street had a statue somewhere. Council seemed to have a constant stream of wealthy donors to fund these installations but they were running out of space, not to mention popular breeds.

Kinney Butterfield took her foot off the gas of the government-owned Prius as she passed a new addition to the City's bronze pack. It was standing in the parking lot outside the Riverdale community center, basking in the last rays of a lovely late May day.

"Check that out," she told her friend Evie Springdale, who was riding shotgun on Kinney's evening shift as a canine corrections officer.

Evie pressed her pale, freckled face to the passenger window. "Is that a mastiff?"

"Dogue de Bordeaux." Kinney slowed even more to let Evie get as good a look as possible in the fading light. "Parents started a petition to have it moved because kids leaving late swimming classes are having nightmares."

"Leave it to Dog Town to take a good thing straight over the top," Evie said, bracing herself on the dash. "Wait a second… What are those smaller figures beside the statue?"

"Puppies." Kinney laughed at Evie's expression. "Instead of moving the statue, Council decided to add a litter to make it kid-friendly. They're our first official bronze puppies."

"Why didn't I know about this?" As the City's former public relations rep, Evie prided herself on knowing everything before it happened. But the halo effect of her short-lived stint seemed to be wearing off. It was hard to keep a high-profile job for long in politics anywhere, but especially in the prickly climate of Dorset Hills.

"Just happened today. The birth announcement hasn't gone out."

Evie craned her neck. "Circle back. I need to take a closer look."

"No can do. I'm on duty, remember? You wanted a ride-along, not a scenic tour."

"But puppies are more important than whatever you have planned."

"More important than a stakeout?" Kinney asked. "I think you underestimate the excitement of my job. I have something big planned for you. Enormous."

Evie sighed and patted the video camera in her lap. "Fine. I'll come back and get some shots of the puppies in daylight."

"You know you can't use that thing tonight, right? This is official City business, and I'm already in Cliff's bad books for getting involved with your show."

"Don't give me all the credit," Evie said. "You had a rep long before I moved here."

Evie was the creative genius behind a new online show called The Princess and the Pig, which profiled Hannah Pemberton, an heiress who had returned to Dorset Hills to rescue a derelict hobby farm. The show had become a viral sensation, much to the dismay of Mayor Bill Bradshaw, who wanted to plow Runaway Farm under and develop the land. He'd lost the war of public opinion, but in the end had managed to save face once again by redrawing the county line so the farm was no longer in his jurisdiction. It seemed like the man had more lives than the cats he was gradually banning from Dorset Hills.

Kinney wasn't so lucky. She'd been caught on camera helping out at the farm, and while her contributions technically didn't cross any professional lines, they put her in the bad books of her boss, Cliff Whorley, the current head of the Canine Corrections Department, or CCD.

"True," she said. "This is just my highest-rated misdemeanor yet."

She continued to drive slowly along the streets of the Riverdale neighborhood, head swivelling left and right. There was always something to see if you looked hard enough. When the town's charm switched off, fascinating mischief turned on.

"Cliff's not the one you need to worry about," Evie said. "You were already on the mayor's hit list when I worked in his office."

"Seriously?" Kinney turned to stare at her. "I should be so far beneath his notice."

"Anyone who so much as smiles at the Rescue Mafia is blackballed," Evie said. "Especially anyone who's friends with Cori Hogan."

The Rescue Mafia was a not-so-secret group of pet rescuers who'd gained notoriety from their daring—and sometimes foolhardy—ploys to protect dogs and embarrass City Council.

"I'd better be more careful," Kinney said. "I really need this job. My head's barely above water after paying down my vet bills from Kali's illness." Her breath caught in her throat as she said the dog's name aloud. Her much-loved golden retriever had died six months earlier from cancer, at the age of six. Kinney had quit her job in the social services department to care for Kali. Afterwards she applied to the CCD to feel like she was working for dogs without actually risking her heart by owning another one. The only good thing that had come of the job so far was that she was temporarily living nearly rent-free in the home of the ousted dog court judge. Marti Forrester had left Dog Town after a political showdown, and was still touring the country with her husband Oliver, and irrepressible dog, Hank.

"Don't worry, the mayor's not paying attention to you right now," Evie said. "He has much bigger challenges than a dog cop with dubious loyalties."

"I do my job well, and it's not easy," Kinney said. She

took pride in walking the fine line between obeying the City's increasingly silly policies around pet citizens and doing the right thing for the animals. If she stepped over that line sometimes, it was always in favor of the animals, and she could sleep at night because of that. But she still needed the job. Without a good reference from the City for her last two jobs, she'd be screwed. "Cori and I are not exactly friends," she added. "Not anymore."

There was an edge of bitterness in her voice. She and Cori had been close friends for years, and had many rescue stories in common. When she accepted the job as a dog cop, however, Cori had practically excommunicated her. Kinney had already backed away from the Mafia when she signed on with municipal social services, but the move to dog cop had destroyed her credibility in Cori's eyes. There was no convincing Cori that there was merit in having someone with the right sentiments *inside* the CCD.

Evie waved away Kinney's protests. "Cori respects you. She was just hurt when you stepped back from the Mafia, and the dog cop role gave her somewhere to focus her rage."

"You know this how?" Kinney asked. "I'm quite sure Cori didn't crack open her hard heart for The Princess and the Pig."

Cori was Dorset Hills' most admired—and feared—dog trainer, and she hadn't achieved that status by oversharing.

"It's in your dossier," Evie said, shrugging.

"My *what?*"

"The Mafia all have files in the mayor's office," Evie said. "Cori, Bridget, Maisie, Nika and Duff. I was assigned to handle you guys, so I made sure to read well."

"I—I don't know what to say." Kinney was actually less embarrassed by having a file than by not knowing about it.

She prided herself on her research and observation skills, and they'd won her the respect of the past judge. But they hadn't kept her out of the dossier of disrespect.

"Don't worry about it," Evie said, pressing her nose to the glass again. She was observant too, and now at liberty to snoop without worrying about her rep. After exposing an exotic pet ring and protecting the mayor from scandal, Evie had escaped relatively unscathed from her stint working for the City, unless you counted a severe concussion. "Like I said, the mayor's focus is elsewhere."

Kinney turned right at the schnauzer statue and left at the vizsla. These days most people navigated the City by the bronze dogs, but that was harder to do with them springing up all over. It seemed like the dogs were becoming less distinctive, too. The artist who had made a killing casting them was probably too exhausted for precision. Now there were three terriers in Riverdale that looked pretty much identical. She'd recently broken up a fistfight between two men over whether the Bedlington terrier was actually a lamb. Next, the wealthy donors who funded these installations would start a petition, too.

"How's your service dog project going?" Kinney asked, just to change the subject.

The glass on Evie's window fogged as she let out a big sigh. "It's not. The mayor's stonewalling because I created the online show. Can't say as I blame him."

"You must be disappointed. It was a great idea."

Evie nodded and then shook her head, summing up her feelings without words. "I made my bed and I don't regret it. Hopefully the next mayor will agree it's a great idea."

"Yeah, but Bill Bradshaw still has three years left in office."

"Maybe," Evie said, fiddling with the controls on her camera.

"Maybe?" Kinney asked.

Evie turned on the video camera and aimed it directly at Kinney. "How's it going between you and James Pemberton?"

"How's *what* going? And turn that thing off. I can't get us to our destination safely if I'm being accosted by paparazzi."

"Nice evasion. It's one of your superpowers." A blazing smile shone out from under the camera. "But it's common knowledge among our viewership that James has the hots for you. Everyone wants to know if you feel the same way."

Kinney checked her mirrors and pulled over so abruptly that Evie's camera wobbled. "Out," she said, putting the car in park. "I can't do my job under these conditions."

Evie lowered the camera. "Oooh, touchy. Someone's got a tragic romantic past she doesn't want to tell the world about."

"Bye-bye, Evie. Hitchhike home if you need to."

Settling back in her seat, Evie crossed her legs. "I know you'd never dump me near the American bulldog bronze. It's a known magnet for Dog Town riffraff."

"Sadly, you're right." Kinney put the car in gear and merged back into traffic. "But I'm a private person and I don't need your viewers speculating on my love life. Not that there's been one for some time." She changed lanes and then changed again. "So there, I said it."

"Well, James would like to do something about that. And if you don't want the sweet, handsome billionaire, I have so many viewers who do."

Slicing an index finger across her throat, Kinney said, "Can we rewind to where you were suggesting the mayor may not last out his term?"

Evie turned, her green eyes gleaming eerily in the light from oncoming cars. "This thing isn't bugged, is it?"

"The Prius? Not that I know of. I guess I should check, given my big fat dossier at City Hall."

Taking a deep breath, Evie said, "Here goes: I want to take the mayor down. And I need you to help me do it."

Kinney pressed the gas instead of the brake and ended up running an amber light. "What? Are you kidding me?"

"Not at all." Evie turned again, leaving Kinney to stare at a mass of red curls. "He's making a mockery of all this wonderful town has become. Good people are leaving and those who stay are revolting over his dog policies. One day the place is going to erupt and everything people have worked for 10 years to build will end."

"Evie." Kinney summoned the calm tone she'd used to talk down hysterical clients when she was in social work. "We can't 'take down' the mayor."

"Why not? Where's your sense of adventure?"

"I think it died with my dog," Kinney said, turning onto a wide street with large, pretty houses. She parked the car along the curb and pushed the seat back. "Like I said, I want to keep my job. I can't be part of any plot to oust the mayor. I'm sorry."

Evie crossed her arms over the camera. "Well, that's a shame, because you're probably in the very best position to help the puppies."

"Puppies? What puppies?"

"Classified. If you're not part of the solution, you're part of the problem."

"Not taking the bait." Kinney reached into the back seat and pulled a set of small binoculars out of her bag. "Whatever you're doing, it's better I don't know about it."

She scanned the dimming street and Evie's head swivelled too. "What are we looking for?"

"You'll know it when you see it. There've been reports of a serious and repeated infraction. I need to catch the perp in the act and then issue a fine."

"Cool," Evie said. "Just when I thought your job was dull."

"It is pretty dull these days. I've been taken off all the high-profile initiatives. Mostly I get grunt work now."

"Then I would think you'd want to help locate the stolen puppies. The ones the mayor told me about and then buried." She caught herself. "I mean he buried the issue, not the puppies. At least, I hope."

Kinney turned quickly and caught the blur of Evie's smirk through the binoculars. "That wasn't fair. You know I can't *unhear* that."

Evie shrugged and stared out the window. "Dogs before all, right?"

"Honestly. What happened to freedom of choice?"

"You gave that up when you bought into the whole idea of Dog Town."

"Are you telling me the truth?" Kinney was still staring at Evie through the binoculars, but it was just a blur. "That the mayor himself told you about stolen puppies?"

"Of course I'm telling you the truth. It happened when he was offering me the job as his chief of staff. But by the time I recovered from my concussion, dealt with Runaway Farm and then started poking around, the problem had disappeared without a trace."

"Stolen puppies are not the kind of problem that would solve itself."

"Exactly. I don't believe it *was* solved. I believe it was

covered up." Evie reached over and pressed the binoculars down. "You're creeping me out with those. And in the meantime, you're missing the guy creeping around with the shovel."

Dropping the binoculars, Kinney reached for the door latch. "That's it, I'm going in. Stay here, and don't you dare use that camera, Evie."

CHAPTER TWO

Kinney's plan had been simply to observe, but the discussion with Evie had riled her up and propelled her out of the car at the first sign of trouble. She hurried along the sidewalk, trying to pull in as many details as she could about the drama that was unfolding. The sun was down but the streetlights flickered on just before she reached the two people arguing on a front lawn.

"This is my property," a woman said. Her voice was so strident that Kinney wanted to turn around and go back to her original plan.

"And I've got more of your property," a man said. "I'm returning it to you."

"You have no evidence that's mine." The strident woman aimed a flashlight and revealed a man holding out a shovel. "Go, before I take matters into my own hands."

"Take *this* into your own hands," he said. "Please."

Sarcasm was the wrong approach to take with someone who was obviously ready to combust with the merest spark. Maybe he wanted her to combust. Some people just liked watching a fire.

There was metallic clatter as the woman moved closer. "I'm warning you, mister. Get off my property."

"I'm *on* my property. That's the whole point. And your property is on my property, so I'm returning it to you. Like a good neighbor."

"Good neighbor? You and your family have been nothing but trouble since you moved in last month. And I've had it, so I'm calling the cops."

Now they were in a circle of light under a street lamp, like a small theater production. Kinney chose that moment to join the play. "Good evening," she said. "The cops have arrived."

The woman appeared to be in her 60s, with wispy grey hair dyed mauve. She held the flashlight in one hand and a garden hoe in the other. Her eyes scanned Kinney and landed on the badge on her tan City uniform.

"I meant real cops," she said. "Not Bill Bradshaw's dog police. You guys are just puppets in his stupid game."

Kinney swallowed hard. Sometimes that was exactly how she felt, but her paycheck depended on taking her role seriously. "Unless I'm much mistaken, ma'am, this is a dog-related matter."

"It's bigger than that. This man intends to violate my property."

Kinney turned to the man. He was probably in his mid-30s and slight, with thinning hair, wire-rimmed glasses and a pale face. His weapon of choice was a shovel, which he held out like an offering.

"Do you see this?" he asked Kinney, brandishing the shovel with its full load.

"I see it, and more importantly, I smell it." She switched instantly to mouth breathing, a dog cop's greatest asset. "Why are you carrying excrement onto this woman's property?"

"I'm simply putting it where it rightfully belongs. She lets her dog crap on my property every day."

Turning back, Kinney asked, "Is this true?"

The woman let her red-framed glasses slide down her nose and stared over them at Kinney. "It most certainly is not, Officer Puppet. My dog defecates on her own property. She's leashed at all times, so I know exactly where and when it happens. But this doofus—who abandons his own dog all day —likes to bring over his own dog's dung and dump it here."

One key to good police work, Kinney had found, was not to follow the crap down the rabbit hole. She had plenty of experience dealing with poop infractions, especially now that she was on Cliff's bad side. It was always about more than the poop.

"All right," she said. "Sounds like there's more at stake than a random dog dump. Sir, can you assure me this poop came from her dog? It must be a very large breed."

He tipped his head toward her house. "She's got a horse in there."

"I have a wolfhound. Your dog is very large, too."

"My dog's a shepherd. His poop is half the size and dry as chalk, because we feed him raw." He waved the shovel around, making even the mauve-haired lady quail from the stink. "You're clearly using some sort of grocery store junk to get this much output."

"What would you know about proper dog care?" she said. "You leave your dog alone all day. My dog has constant company."

"Constant company with a lunatic. How is that better?"

"Young man, you're the one about to put dog poop in my new mailbox. How is that sane?"

Kinney stepped forward and faced the man with the shovel. "Were you going to put poop in her mailbox?"

His thin lips pursed before he spoke. "Technically not."

"Explain the technicality," she said.

He nodded to the mailbox, which appeared to be freshly installed given that the dirt was light and dusty at its base. Plastic flowers and dog figurines were glued to the silver metal box, which read, "Myrtle McCabe."

"She installed it last week on *my* side of the property line. Clearly the work of a lunatic."

"I see," Kinney said. "So what's really at stake is the property line."

"We had the land assessed recently so that we could build a new fence," he said. "Tall fences make good neighbors, right?"

"So I've heard." Kinney smiled for the first time, but the second she let her guard down, the smell crept in. It was certainly a foul load, and she'd sniffed a lot of them.

"But Mrs. McCabe disputed the assessment. She planted a garden on my side years ago and doesn't want to lose it."

"I don't want to lose it because it's mine," Mrs. McCabe said. "You must have bought off Bill Bradshaw's lackeys to redraw property lines that have existed for sixty years."

"I didn't buy off anyone," he said. "This is my land, fair and square, and you can't park your stupid mailbox on it or let your dog crap over here."

"And you can't dig up my flowers and dump them on the lawn to die." Mrs. McCabe gestured to a row of unearthed plants sitting outside the circle of light. "I got those calla lilies from my grandmother. They're Dorset Hills heritage plants."

Kinney positioned herself directly between the shovel and the hoe. "Did you dump her plants?"

"I asked her to dig them up herself. We're getting the yard fenced later this week. When she didn't answer I figured I was doing her a favor."

The truth was usually somewhere in the middle, just as Kinney was now. "I've got an idea. How about you both put your weapons down and we'll go inside to discuss this calmly? The neighbors are watching."

"What else is new?" the man said. "They've been spying on me and reporting to Lady McCabe."

"It's just our Neighborhood Pooch Patrol. We all watch out for each other," she said. "And everyone's worried about how you treat your dog, Dan Barber."

Dan cursed and pulled the full shovel back, preparing to swing. Mrs. McCabe swung her hoe back, too. Kinney decided a second too late to move and what happened next was a blur. She was hit once, twice, three times and fell onto the grass. Rolling onto her back, she found herself staring into Evie Springdale's camera.

The camera tipped up and swivelled. "Back off. Everyone. You're currently being filmed for an episode of The Princess and the Pig. I suggest you get yourselves—and that dog—inside pronto or risk national ridicule."

There was a shuffle in the darkness and then silence. Evie lowered the camera and offered her hand to Kinney. Shaking her head, Kinney got up on her own. "Don't touch me. I'm covered in dog crap."

"Believe it or not, I've smelled and touched worse," Evie said. "Shooting at Runaway Farm is no bed of roses. Are you hurt?"

Kinney shook herself off. "Nothing serious. Hit me in the hip with the shovel and my shin with the hoe." Picking up a stick, she scraped off some of the stinky residue. "He's not wrong about inferior poop quality. It makes a good case for raw feeding."

Evie pulled out her phone and turned on the flashlight. "Kinney, your arm's bleeding."

"It is?" Kinney looked at her wrist. "It looks like a bite. Did you mention a dog?"

Evie nodded. "Looked like a shepherd."

"Damn. I was hoping it was the wolfhound, so I could fine our lady of the crazy mailbox."

"I bet you can find another reason to fine her," Evie said. "Let's go interview them."

Kinney looked down at her filthy uniform and shook her head. "Rule number one of mediation is wait till cooler heads prevail. Mine and theirs."

"Rule number one of reality shows: strike while the iron is hot, and light a fire if you need to keep it that way."

"Evie. You can't use that footage."

She shrugged. "We know that, but they don't. I guarantee neither of them wants this stupidity to air so they'll be motivated tonight to cooperate. Wait till tomorrow and they'll figure out I need waivers."

"Okay." Kinney straightened her shoulders and walked toward Dan Barber's house. "But this is a crazy way to do business."

"This is crazy business, period. There were no duels over poop with garden equipment before Bill Bradshaw took office. What we have here is a clash of the old guard and the new. Mailbox Myrtle gave that away with her Officer Puppet comment, which is actually pretty clever."

Glancing over her shoulder, Kinney said, "I take it you completely ignored my order to stay in the car."

"I saw a chance to get the real poop on Dog Town politics."

"This is bigger than poop now, Evie. Much bigger. I got bitten, and there's zero tolerance for that even with dog court suspended."

Evie nodded. "It's no laughing matter, I get it. But you'd

better stop saying 'poop' if you want them to take you seriously."

"What do you prefer? Dung? Manure?" Kinney rubbed her hip as they went up Dan Barber's stairs. It wasn't the worst case she'd handled—not by far—but she had a sick feeling in her stomach that only partly came from the stench.

"Try shizzle," Evie suggested. "It has pizzazz."

"Right, because that's what I'm looking for here: pizzazz."

"It never hurts, Kinney. You really need to kick up those work boots more often."

"Maybe when I recover from my injuries. In the meantime, follow my lead."

Evie was already several steps ahead of her. "Got it."

CHAPTER THREE

The door opened even before they knocked and a tired-looking woman welcomed them inside. "I'm so sorry," she said. "I'm Ginny Barber, and you met my husband, Dan. I'm afraid things came to a head with Mrs. McCabe tonight. Dan would like to apologize for—" She covered her nose and averted her eyes. "Everything."

Dan came out of the kitchen, looking more defiant than contrite. "I am sorry," he said. "For hitting *you* with the load of crap and not Lunatic McCabe. Waste of good ammo. But no doubt she'll leave more tomorrow. Her dog's a producer."

"Dan!" His wife gave him a reproachful look and then gestured to the floor. A boy of about eight was sitting cross-legged with a beautiful German shepherd beside him, its long black nose resting on his leg.

The dog looked familiar, but Kinney supposed most shepherds looked more or less the same. This one had beautiful, intense eyes, but a thin crescent of white showed, as if he were frightened. There was no visible threat but the house pulsated with enough energy to raise the hair on her arms.

Something felt wrong here, and it was about more than a crazy mailbox.

"Are you going to report us?" Ginny asked. "I'm sure there are worse issues than a disagreement over dog poop."

"Much worse," Kinney said. There was something likeable about the woman, and the kid looked sweet. "I'm sure we can sort that out among ourselves. What I'm more concerned about is this."

She lifted her sleeve and showed the twin punctures on either side of her forearm.

"Oh my gosh," Ginny said. "Did Whiskey do that?"

Her husband stepped forward for a closer look and then shook his head. "That was McCabe's hoe."

Kinney stared at him. "Dan, these marks would fit Whiskey's fangs like Cinderella's slipper."

He shrugged. "Take the dog, then. He's more trouble than he's worth."

"No, Daddy!" The little boy hugged the dog, which huddled in closer. "I love Whiskey."

"It's okay, Liam," Ginny said. "Daddy doesn't mean it."

Dan flung himself into a battered leather chair. "You agreed to take the dog while your sister's on tour, Ginny. I didn't. The dog was fine when he got here but lately he's jumpy as hell and now he's bitten a dog cop. This is more dog than we can handle. Let Jacinda handle this."

"Jacinda Allen?" Kinney said. "I met her back in January, when she was leaving on a road trip with the dog."

Ginny's face brightened. "You know my sister? That's amazing. Her music took off and she got a chance to open for a band on a European tour. She was going to leave Whiskey with her mother-in-law but when that fell through, I offered to do it. Jacinda's married now, you know. A stop in Vegas took care of that."

"How wonderful," Kinney said, smiling. "And your son obviously loves Whiskey."

"That makes one of us," Dan piped up. "Old Lady McCabe isn't wrong about the dog being alone too long when we're working."

"That's why we put in the dog door," Ginny said. "He can go in and out when he wants. Jacinda said he did just fine for nine hours on his own."

Kinney eyed Dan, wondering if he was the source of the bad energy in the house. Whiskey had had plenty of upheaval this year, leaving home on a road trip with his owner and then getting offloaded here. Now there was tension with the neighbor on top of everything.

"I know this is a good dog," Kinney said. "I'd like to give him a second chance, even though it goes against CCD policy."

"Thank you," Ginny said, Liam's higher voice overlapping hers.

"But you're going to have to end the battle with Mrs. McCabe," she said.

Dan glowered. "It's my property. I have the survey to prove it."

"But she thought it was hers for decades. Give her a chance to adjust without throwing her plants all over. They're probably like pets to her. I'm sure you can understand that."

"Not really," Dan said, crossing his arms. "She's nuts."

Evie stepped around Kinney with her camera. "I'm just a bystander, but I can't help saying you came off looking worse than she did. Most people learn not to throw poop as kids."

"Evie," Kinney said.

"Hey, you're in that show," Ginny said. "The Princess and the Pig. I love it!"

"Why, thank you." Evie grinned at Kinney. "You guys should come out to Runaway Farm one day. It would be good for Dan to watch the goats play. Very therapeutic."

"I don't think so," Dan said, over Liam's eager clamor. He got up from his chair and opened the door. "You'll want to get over to Old Lady McCabe's before lights out at nine."

As they walked across the lawn, Kinney said, "You promised to keep quiet."

"That's before I knew Dan was a complete jerk. He needed a dose of public shaming. I worry about his kid."

"I worry about Whiskey," Kinney said. "That dog was perfectly sound when I met him in January. If he's biting, something has gone far wrong."

She hadn't expected a crowd, but Mrs. McCabe had summoned three neighbors during the time they were with the Barbers.

"Ladies, come in," she said, pleasantly. "I hope you don't mind but the Neighborhood Pooch Patrol wanted to meet you. I've made tea and Gertie Oakley brought over some cookies."

"That's so nice," Kinney said. "Dog cops don't get that kind of welcome often." She glanced at Evie and smirked. "Oh wait, it's your camera they want to meet."

Mrs. McCabe waved the comment away. "Don't be silly. We got off to a rocky start, that's all. I'm sure you see that Dan Barber is bad news. I'm not the only neighbor he's turned against."

"She's right," said Addie Linton, a small, round woman with mild blue eyes and platinum curls. "He's always complaining about something. These newcomers to Dorset Hills want to be coddled."

Liza Northcott, a tall woman with her hair in a silver bun nodded agreement. "They act so entitled, when really we're all in this together. It's about being good dog owners and neighbors. How difficult is that?"

A shaggy wolfhound on a massive dog bed in the corner lifted its head to look at them as if in agreement.

"I'd like to hear more," Kinney said, "but do you mind if I wash my hands, first?"

"Of course," Mrs. McCabe said, pointing out the way to the kitchen. Then she ushered Evie to the best seat in the house, an overstuffed floral recliner. "Tell us all about Hannah Pemberton," she said, pouring tea out of a china pot. "Is she really together with that handsome Nick?"

Evie slipped the camera under her arm so that she could take the tea cup. "I can assure you it's true... because Nick is my brother. There's never been a sweeter couple, really."

Kinney left them chatting and gave the wound on her arm a thorough wash with dish soap at the kitchen sink. She dried it with a handful of tissues and examined it. It wasn't that bad. If Whiskey had really wanted to bite someone, it would have been much worse than four small punctures.

When she bent over to pick up a stray tissue she noticed four red canisters lined up against the wall beside a big bag of potting soil. Pulling out her phone she took a photo, and then stuffed the blood-tinged tissues into her uniform pocket.

Back in the living room, she said, "Mrs. McCabe, would you mind if I came back tomorrow after a shower and change of clothes? Really, I can't even stand the smell myself, so I'm sure the Pooch Patrol feels the same."

"Dear, sit down right here." She gestured to a kitchen chair covered by a green garbage bag. "Have some tea."

"Please don't go so soon," Addie said. "I'm still hoping to hear about Evie's handsome Jon. I always dreamed about marrying a veterinarian."

"Actually, I've been called away," Kinney said. "I'll be

back tomorrow, and if Evie's free, I'm sure she'll come with me."

"Absolutely," Evie said. "I enjoy following Mayor Bradshaw's puppets around."

"Oh, Evie," Mrs. McCabe said. "That came out all wrong, earlier. I can see Officer Butterfield is just doing her job. It's not easy keeping the peace in Dog Town, is it?"

"It certain isn't," Kinney said. "Just gets more complicated by the day."

Mrs. McCabe took the cup and saucer from Evie. "I'd love to come out to the farm one day."

Evie looked at Kinney and then smiled. "Let's talk about it tomorrow, ladies. I hope there's some of those cookies left."

CHAPTER FOUR

"Dog bites are serious business," Mim Gardiner said, her dark hair gleaming under the overhead lights as she examined Kinney's arm with a magnifying glass the next day. "You really should get this checked out."

Kinney pulled her stool closer to Mim's kitchen island. "I am getting it checked out... by a nurse with a magnifying glass and half a dozen disinfectants. I highly doubt it could be cleaner than it is."

Mim angled Kinney's forearm to the right and left, and then sighed. "Fangs can drive bacteria right into the wound. Did you at least clean it quickly?"

"She did," Evie said. She was perched on the island itself, kicking her heels. Her red curls were smooth and loose today, and she was wearing pink high-heeled sandals that showed off a pedicure that sparkled like opals. "She skulked off to the kitchen leaving me with the Pooch Patrol."

"Pooch Patrol?" The voice came from the stool next to Kinney's. Arianna Torrance, a successful breeder of high-end goldendoodle hybrids, and Mim's best friend, had come by to spend a rare day off. Like many of the women in their circles,

Mim and Ari worked constantly, partly to earn flexibility to be available at the drop of a hat to help a friend or dog in need. Kinney frequently picked up extra shifts, too, both for the cash and because she hoped to get some of the more interesting cases. So far, only the cash had been forthcoming.

"It's like a neighborhood watch group made up of older women," Kinney said. "From what I can tell, they're mainly ratting out people who aren't onside with old-school values. They keep the Tattletail Hotline busy. Now I've figured out why so many of our calls are over here in Riverdale. They walk their dogs and snoop."

"Poor Whiskey," Evie said. "For all their bleating about the mayor's policies, that dog's going to be their next victim."

"Do they know about the bite?" Mim asked.

Kinney shook her head. "I hid the evidence, and the Barbers won't mention it."

"Dan might," Evie said. "He seemed eager to be rid of Whiskey."

"That dog is one of the brightest I've seen, and he has a huge heart," Kinney said, pulling her arm away from Mim and getting up to pace. "I need to do something to fix this."

"What did you have in mind?" Ari's blue eyes widened with concern. She twisted her long blonde hair into a bun and wove two chopsticks from Chinese takeout through it. "Can I help?"

She was part of the extended group of friends associated with the Rescue Mafia, but not quite part of the inner sanctum. Cori Hogan and Bridget Linsmore kept membership locked down pretty tight. Many hands made light work; many lips could allow secrets to slip.

And there were so many secrets. Even Kinney, a professional keeper of secrets, had trouble keeping track.

"First, I've got research to do," Kinney said. "I have my

suspicions about what's been going on—beyond the obvious. Whiskey was a sensitive dog even before getting dumped on Dan Barber. I remember he looked at his owner, Jacinda, as if she were the only person on the planet. You don't see that kind of devotion all the time."

"True," Ari said. "I breed my hybrids to be happy-go-lucky and love everyone. But sometimes I miss the single-minded devotion a shepherd brings."

Evie plucked orange hairs off her black skirt. "It's like you guys are speaking another language. Cat lover here."

"I've never known the love of a good shepherd either," Mim said, grinning as she left the kitchen. George, the doodle hybrid Ari had bred for her, didn't move from the back door, where he was watching squirrels.

"I've got a little situation to chat about, too," Evie said, as Mim came back with a basket of bandages of all shapes and sizes. "Stolen puppies."

"Evie!" Kinney resisted as Mim tried to grab her arm. "That's classified."

"Yeah, I classified it last night when you weren't interested. Now you're interested so I'm tabling it." She slapped the marble counter beside her. "Ari is going to want to know."

"About stolen puppies?" Ari said. "Damn straight."

Evie hopped down and turned. "When Mayor Bradshaw visited my place after we busted the exotic pet ring, he told me some puppies had gone missing and were presumed stolen. He said Leann Cosgrove lost a beagle and Ruth Banks a Maltese. At that point, about a dozen breeders had lost a single dog."

"What? Why didn't Leann and Ruth mention this to me?" Ari said. "I've seen them a couple of times since then to discuss City Hall's regulations for breeders."

"Good question," Evie said. "Even if they got their puppies back they'd have mentioned it, right?"

"I certainly hope so. If it could happen to them, it could happen to anyone." Ari pulled the chopsticks out of her hair and it fell like spun gold. Flynn Strathmore, Dog Town's most notable cartoonist, often drew Ari as an angel and once you'd seen that, it was hard to see her any other way. "There's something funny going on."

"I told you so, Kinney," Evie said. "There's a mystery stirring and you don't want to rock the boat."

"I said I don't want to lose my job." Kinney watched as Mim covered the dog bite with a flesh-colored bandage. "I was unemployed for months last year and it terrified me."

"I understand," Evie said. "Technically I'm unemployed right now. But I got fired so many times from political jobs that I made sure to save while I could. That gives me some freedom now to—"

"To be a thorn in the mayor's side?" Kinney interrupted, grinning.

Evie turned her intense green stare on Kinney. "To do something right after all the wrong things I had to do in my career."

Kinney met her eyes and nodded. "Okay."

"Luckily, I don't have a job to lose, per se," Ari said. "At this point my dogs pretty much sell themselves." She got off the stool and put her hands on her hips. "Come to think of it... why hasn't one of my dogs been stolen?"

"George got stolen," Mim said. "Was that scary enough?"

"That was different," Ari said. "What I mean is, why did the puppy thief overlook mine? I have a waiting list a year long and charge way more than Leann Cosgrove and Ruth Banks."

"The mayor said only purebreds went missing," Evie told her. "It sounds like the thief is elitist."

Ari pulled lipstick out of her purse and applied it without a mirror. "I don't know whether to be relieved or insulted. I've had purebred snobs diss my dogs for a decade and finally crossbreeding is working in my favor."

"So far," Evie said. "Until we know the full story I'd keep those pups on lockdown."

Mim ran her fingers around the bandage to seal it and said, "Kinney, make sure you take this off when you're at home so it can breathe. Dog bites are vulnerable to infection. But visible dog bites are vulnerable to gossip."

"Understood," Kinney said. "And thank you."

"We need to talk to Cori about this situation," Ari said.

"I don't want her to know I got bitten," Kinney said. "She'll tell me I should have seen it coming."

"The dog wasn't even visible," Evie said. "How could you see it coming?"

"A dog cop should anticipate that where there's a dog problem, there might be a problem dog."

"I didn't mean that anyway," Ari said. "I meant we should call a Mafia 911 about the missing puppies. Why haven't you told her already, Evie?"

"I'd checked in with the mayor and he said it was nothing. Then it kind of slipped my mind with all the fuss about Runaway Farm." She tapped her red curls. "Head injury, remember? But it still kept nagging at me, so I decided to do some digging before letting Cori get worked up. Who knows, there might be a logical explanation for all of it."

Ari took out another tube of lipstick and applied a second coat. "You worked in the mayor's office during breeder-gate. Do you really think there's anything logical about this?"

Evie shook her head. "That's why I enlisted the best investigator I know."

"Aw, thanks," Kinney said, rolling down her sleeve. "You've just earned yourself another ride-along."

"YOU SAID A RIDE-ALONG, NOT A CRAWL-ALONG," Evie grumbled from the long grass in the field behind the McCabe and Barber houses. "I have allergies, Kinney. I can't roll in pollen without breaking out in hives."

"Just give it a few more minutes," Kinney said, wiping perspiration from her brow. She didn't know whether it was from the lovely spring day or nerves. "Whiskey's got to come out soon."

"The least you could have done is warn me to dress properly. Ants are biting my toes."

"I did say there might be rough terrain. Besides, I'm not really on duty."

"This is how you spend your free time?"

"I like to stay busy," Kinney said. "There's always something interesting happening around town."

Evie adjusted the camera. "I'm going to film this whether you like it or not. My spidey sense tells me something is going very wrong around here."

"My spidey sense agrees."

Evie shuffled over about six inches and adjusted her camera again. "I only joined you last night to talk about the missing puppies, by the way. Who said anything about becoming your unpaid backup?"

"Who said anything about unpaid? In exchange for your excellent company I'll provide you with many hours of free expert sleuthing."

"Well, that's different, then." Evie sniffled and blinked her rapidly reddening eyes. "But you indicated I was in the way last night."

"On the contrary, you were a big help with Mrs. McCabe and the starstruck Pooch Patrol. If I'm going back in today, I want you as my wing-woman."

"Well, I always sensed I was wasted in public relations, but who knew my real calling was undercover police work? I busted the exotic pet ring and now this."

"First rule of undercover, Evie? Silence."

Evie stared through her viewfinder. "Luckily, Whiskey is joining us now."

The plastic dog door lifted and a long black nose appeared underneath. The big dog paused for what seemed like ages before emerging. Then he skulked across the dog run with his belly close to the ground. Just as he was maneuvering into position to lift his leg, there was a sharp sound like a firecracker.

Evie and Kinney both flinched and gasped.

The sound came again. The dog was frozen with his leg partially raised. With the third "shot" he fled back into the house without doing his business.

"Was that an air gun?" Evie said, finally looking away from the camera. "The poor dog was terrified. He couldn't pee... and I almost did."

"I'm not sure," Kinney said. "It was coming from the direction of the McCabe house. The timing can't be a coincidence."

"Air guns aren't legal in city limits," Evie said. "The only time loud noises are permitted are for fireworks on the Fourth of July. Even then, it's controversial."

Kinney sighed. "If I didn't know Mrs. McCabe is a

founding member of the Pooch Patrol, I'd say she's deliberately terrorizing that dog."

Evie's eyes watered instantly, and not from allergies. "She can't be. That would be cruel."

"We'll need proof," Kinney said. "Let me think for a second."

She was still gathering her wits when there was a crackle behind them. They both rolled over and Evie yanked down her skirt. Standing a few yards away was a boy in a baseball cap, with a backpack almost as big as he was.

"Oh, hey Liam," Kinney said, propping herself up on one arm. "Home from school early?"

He nodded, his dark eyes pleading. "Don't tell my mom."

"Of course not," Evie said, brushing dirt, leaves and twigs off her clothes. "This can be our little secret."

"Agreed," Kinney said. "As long as you tell us what's going on. Is someone picking on you at school?"

Liam shook his head. "I think someone's picking on Whiskey. When I come home from school he's always shaking and whining. He didn't used to do that."

"Ah," Kinney said, getting to her feet. "It's nice that you care about that dog so much."

"I love him," Liam said, shrugging off his backpack. "But he makes my dad yell all the time. More than usual."

Evie took Kinney's hand and wobbled onto her high heels. "It sounds tough at home right now, buddy."

He adjusted his baseball cap to shield his eyes. "I hate this house."

Kinney took a card out of her pocket and slipped it into his hand. "I want you to go inside and give Whiskey a big hug for me, okay. That's what your Aunt Jacinda would want you to do. She loves that dog. We're going to come visit your parents in a little while. But I want you to put this card someplace safe, and know that you can always call me if you're upset about anything. Okay?"

He nodded and started walking through the field toward the house. After a few yards, he turned back. "You making a movie?"

"Something like that," Evie said.

"I hope it's fun," he said, looking like he needed a laugh.

"It's going to have a happy ending," Kinney said. "That's the only kind of movie we like."

CHAPTER FIVE

"I t's a good thing you're with me or I might lose my cool," Kinney said, as they walked up Myrtle McCabe's front stairs.

"I got your back, partner," Evie said. "If I can handle Mayor Bradshaw, I can handle the Pooch Patrol."

Letting her sunglasses slide down her nose, Kinney stared at her. "I could have sworn you said Mayor Bradshaw beat you at your own game with Runaway Farm."

Evie shrugged and grinned. "Well, I underestimated him, but I won't make the same mistake again."

She handed Kinney the camera so that she could twist her curls into a neat knot. Then she smoothed her clothes. Even after rolling around in a field she managed to look more polished than Kinney ever felt.

"Just do like we discussed, okay?" Kinney said. "Turn on the charm and the camera. Keep them busy while I snoop around."

She rang the doorbell. Myrtle McCabe peeked through floral curtains and was already on the phone by the time she opened the door. "How nice to see you, girls! Do come in. I'll put on a pot of tea right away."

"I hope you're ready for your close-up today," Evie said. "I want to hear more about this Pooch Patrol and I'm ready to roll camera."

"Just give me a chance to put on my lipstick," Mrs. McCabe said, running her hands over her flyaway mauve hair.

"Absolutely," Evie said, heading for the cushy recliner.

Kinney perched on the arm of the couch and watched as Gertie, Addie and Liza streamed in and gathered around Evie, signing waivers and talking over each other. After Mrs. McCabe brought in a tray of tea and cookies, Kinney slipped away to the kitchen. She washed her hands quickly and then got down on one knee.

The red cans that had been lined up beside the potting soil were gone.

Sitting back on her heels, she opened the cupboard under the sink. Inside she found only the usual cleaning supplies. She tried the next cupboard, and the rattle of the pots and lids must have masked Mrs. McCabe's footsteps.

"Kinney, can I help you with something?"

She rose to face her host. "So sorry, Mrs. McCabe, I was just looking for— Oh, there." She pointed to a hint of red hidden in a long curtain at the sliding glass door and walked towards it. "I just wanted to check that out."

Mrs. McCabe moved surprisingly quickly for her age. Gardening had obviously kept her in good shape. But Kinney was faster.

"Give me that," Mrs. McCabe said, trying to pry the red can out of Kinney's fingers.

Kinney backed away and raised one knee, fending off

Mrs. McCabe and her wolfhound, Heidi, who'd decided to investigate.

"You must have gotten a great deal on canned air, Mrs. McCabe. I saw four canisters beside the potting soil last night."

"So?" Mrs. McCabe's hands were on the hips of her billowing drawstring pants.

"This product is banned in Dorset Hills now. It's like fireworks in a can, and not at all dog-friendly."

"It works like a charm to deter barking," Mrs. McCabe said, with a bland smile. "We keep a peaceful neighborhood here."

Kinney peered out the back door. She could see Whiskey's wire mesh dog run clearly through the sparse hedge. No wonder the Barbers wanted a better fence.

"Whiskey definitely wasn't barking when you used this half an hour ago. He'd just come out to do his business and you terrified him so much he shot back inside."

"I did no such thing." Mrs. McCabe's tone was defiant, but she lowered her voice so her friends couldn't hear. Obviously she was working alone.

"I have proof, actually," Kinney said.

"You're spying on me?"

"I have a personal interest in Whiskey, and I can't tell you how upsetting it was to see him cringe and run. That sound is torture for a sensitive dog. How do you manage to fire off canned air without startling your own dog? She must have nerves of steel."

The woman's eyes dropped, and she ran her hand over the dog's bristly grey head. "Deaf. Still doesn't like the vibrations."

"Mrs. McCabe. You seem like a dog lover. I don't understand how you could willingly inflict pain on Whiskey."

"It's not about Whiskey. It's about Dan Barber. He doesn't belong in this neighborhood, and we'd like him to leave."

Kinney leaned against the counter and counted to five. Anger would scorch her tongue with furious words if she weren't careful. Sometimes people just didn't realize the impact of their actions after emotion took over. She couldn't help this woman understand if she lost her own temper.

"I won't argue that Dan seems difficult. But you're punishing the dog, not the man. Whiskey is traumatized and acting strangely because of what you're doing. I knew this dog before the Barbers took him. He had a solid temperament, which you're destroying pretty quickly."

"I'm sure Dan Barber destroyed his temperament more than a few puffs of air ever could."

Kinney counted to five again more slowly. "I know it was more than that. There's at least one witness who's commented on the noise." She pushed herself off the counter. "I'll bet the Pooch Patrol have heard strange daytime explosions, too. Let's ask."

"No!" Mrs. McCabe caught her arm. "There's no need for them to know any of this. You have no proof."

"Oh, but we do." The voice was cool but light. Kinney turned and found the round eye of Evie's camera trained on them. "Take a look at the dirt on my skirt and the bites on my legs. It was one heck of a stakeout."

"I want you and that camera out of my house." Mrs. McCabe advanced on Evie, with the wolfhound by her side. Heidi might be deaf, but she was a good enough judge of body language that her hackles rose.

"What's going on?" The other members of the Pooch Patrol were standing in the kitchen doorway. Liza was wearing a taupe wrap that was as elegant as her silvery bun. "Myrtle, you seem flustered."

"I—I am. It turns out these ladies are here doing Bill Bradshaw's dirty work."

"How so?" asked Addie. "Evie's show has stuck it to the mayor. These girls seem too sensible to support Bill's foolishness."

"You're right," Evie said. "I do try to stick it to the mayor whenever I can. But I'm a freelancer, now. Kinney is on the municipal payroll so she has to follow the rules, at least most of the time."

"That must be difficult, Officer Butterfield," Addie said.

Kinney nodded. "Nothing is black and white. Where pets are concerned, sometimes good people do bad things and vice versa."

"Sounds complicated," Addie said. "Life in Dorset Hills used to be simpler."

"Agreed," Kinney said. "And I know it's been tough for everyone to adjust." She turned to Mrs. McCabe. "I like to give people the benefit of the doubt. So how about we let the dust settle and I'll come around in few days and see how you and the Barbers are getting on?"

Mrs. McCabe gave a pained smile. "Lovely. I'll be too busy replanting my garden to have time for Dan's foolishness."

"Good," Kinney said, beckoning to Evie. "I'm heading over to broker peace with him now."

Addie Linton followed so close on Kinney's heels that she accidentally kicked the older woman. At the door, she pressed a business card into Kinney's hand. "If you happen to need an expert dog-sitter, I come very well recommended."

"Good to know," Kinney said, slipping it into her pocket. "Although I don't have a dog."

"You will," Addie said. "People like you never last long without a dog."

Kinney's eyebrows rose. "People like me?"

Addie nodded, her sharp eyes glinting. "The good people. There are still a few of us left in Dog Town."

DAN BARBER SCOWLED when he saw the camera, even though it was dangling from Evie's right hand. "You two again?"

"Good evening," Kinney said. "May we come in?"

"No. We're just about to eat dinner."

"Dan!" His wife sounded horrified as she nudged him out of the doorway. "We just got home and I haven't even started cooking. Kinney, of course you can come in. You're always welcome here. I spoke to my sister today and she remembers you fondly."

Kinney didn't wait for Dan's next salvo, pushing past him with Evie close on the heels of her City-issued work boots. "I won't keep you long. Just wanted to have a quick chat about your doggie door. I'm not sure if you're aware they're against city regulations."

"I had no idea," Ginny said. "Why would that be against regulations?"

"Dogs can get into trouble when they're out unsupervised. You'd be surprised."

Still in the front entrance, Dan crossed his arms. "Have you been spying on us?"

Kinney shrugged. "Just doing my due diligence after the fracas last night. The empty lot behind you is City property."

"How convenient." Dan retreated to his leather chair as

Liam crept in. The boy met Kinney's eyes for a second and nodded, accepting her silent request to stay quiet.

"We have nothing to hide," Ginny said. "We thought we were doing something nice for Whiskey. He can get some fresh air while we're at work."

"Except that I've heard complaints about random sounds in this neighborhood," Kinney said. "Something like fire-crackers. I heard it today and saw Whiskey flinch when he was outside. Last night I noticed he wasn't the calm dog I met five months ago. That may be one reason why."

"What are the City's regulations on fireworks?" Dan asked.

"Also banned. Along with any loud noises that would terrify dogs." She looked down at Whiskey, who was once again lying with his long muzzle on Liam's leg. A shudder washed over him, from flattened ears to tail. "He seems distressed."

Ginny's forehead creased in worry. "He's been shaking a lot lately. I thought he just missed my sister."

"I'm sure that's also true. Stress can have serious reper-cussions for dogs." She held out her arm and the cuff of her jacket slid up to reveal the bandage. "And for humans. You'll need to do some work to desensitize him and reverse the damage. I can recommend an expert trainer."

Dan straightened from his slouch. "We'll surrender the dog."

Ginny and Liam both gasped. "We can't give away my sister's dog," Ginny said.

"She left him with us and he bit a dog cop, Ginny. Now he's apparently traumatized and neither one of us has the time or skill to 'desensitize' him. What if he bit Liam next?"

"Whiskey would never bite me, Daddy. He's my best friend."

The dog literally wormed his way into the boy's lap and managed to flip over onto his back, the very image of submission.

A familiar feeling stirred in Kinney's heart. It was grief over the loss of Kali. She'd worked so hard to process it, but zigzagged perpetually through the anger and depression stages. She would never get to acceptance. That her dog could be taken so early was impossible to accept.

Clenching her fists, she drove her nails into her palms. It was almost always enough to keep tears at bay. She had a high threshold to start with, thanks to her stint in social services, where she frequently encountered families far more fraught than this one.

"Abandoning the dog now will only increase his stress, Dan. The trainer I mentioned can come here to work with you and I'm sure it's nothing the three of you can't handle, working together."

Dan shook his head. "It's too risky, especially with that Pooch Patrol crawling all over. If it got out that Whiskey bit a dog cop it would make us look bad. Ginny works in a child care center. Imagine if he bit a child?"

"I'll do the work, Dan," Ginny said. "Liam and I can make it a project."

"Yeah, Daddy." Liam hugged the dog as best he could. "We'll fix Whiskey so he isn't scared anymore."

Dan just shook his head again. "I have to do what's best for our family. Someday maybe we'll get a smaller dog. After Old Lady McCabe dies." He turned to Kinney. "Take him tonight. No use prolonging it."

She waited a moment for the lump in her throat to subside. "Dan, this dog won't do well in Animal Services. The noise and confusion would overwhelm him." She raised her hand before he could respond. "Plus the City doesn't look kindly on reactive dogs."

"Not my problem. We took the dog in and if the worst thing we did was give him a dog door, I can live with that." He turned to walk into the kitchen. "Liam, don't. Sometimes things aren't fair. The sooner you learn that, the better."

Tears rolled down Liam's face as he looked up at Kinney. "Can't you take him? You'll fix him and maybe we can have him back."

"Whisky should at least be returned to Jacinda, when she's back," Ginny said, kneeling beside Liam. "She'll be so upset about all this. But I'm sure she'd be relieved to think he's in your capable hands."

"Me?" Kinney was shaking her head even as the word came out. "I can't. I'm barely at home. Plus, it's against the rules of my job."

Liam's big eyes turned to Evie and she said, "No can do. I'm allergic." She wiped her eyes, which were streaming from more than animal dander. "Kinney, can't we, you know, do something? We know people."

Kinney stared down at the big dog, still on his back in Liam's lap. The dog looked back, and a strange feeling tingled in her spine. She had never seen such intelligent eyes in a dog's face. They seemed almost human. In fact, they were more human than the eyes of many people she'd met, and eyes like that should never be behind bars in Animal Services... or worse.

"Okay," she told Liam. "I will look out for Whiskey. Just like I did with your aunt. He is a special dog."

Ginny hugged her, and now the only dry eyes in the room were Kinney's, unless you counted Whiskey's. Liam pushed the dog out of his lap and came over to wrap his arms around Kinney's waist.

"Promise?" he asked.

She nodded, and when he squeezed her harder the word came out. "Promise."

Dan cleared his throat as he came back in with the leash. "Good luck with that. He's not coming back here. Ever."

Kinney glared at him before disengaging herself from Liam and bending to hook up the dog. A long nose poked into her hair and the dog licked her ear. "It's okay, buddy," she whispered. "I got you."

She avoided looking at Liam sobbing in Ginny's arms as she left. It was something she'd witnessed too often in social work...something she'd hoped never to see again when she left that job behind. Being a dog cop was supposed to be easier, but it wasn't working out that way.

Outside on the porch, Evie lowered her camera. "That was awful. Awful! One day we need to expose the seedy underbelly of Dog Town, where people traumatize dogs and give them up, all because of politics."

Kinney blew her hair back from her forehead, which had beaded with perspiration. It wasn't all from stress: the humidity had crept in today and soon summer would hit full force.

"I can't keep this dog, Evie. I'd lose my job for concealing a biter, no doubt about that."

"I've got it all on video, remember? The dog didn't really bite. It was just a drive-by nip and your arm got in the way."

"He was very likely going for Myrtle McCabe and her garden hoe, but aggression is aggression." Kinney said. "Anyway, Cliff won't buy any of it. I'll need to get Cori and Bridget to place Whiskey with someone who knows how to work with dogs like this."

The dog nuzzled her hand as she led him to the car, and

when she looked up, Evie's smile was like the sun coming out from behind a cloud. "Like the bad man said, good luck with that."

CHAPTER SIX

When Kinney first laid eyes on Runaway Farm, it had resembled something out of an old western ghost town. The house and the outbuildings were crumbling and there seemed to be a perpetual cloud of dust blowing up in little eddies. The previous owner's money had all gone into maintaining his rescue animals, which had included an old blind horse, cows, sheep, a parrot, and a small terrier with a big attitude, named Prima. Hannah Pemberton, the heiress who'd come home to Dorset Hills from New York City, bought the farm and started refurbishing it. The mayor had fought her every step of the way, because he'd slated the land for development. Finally, the dust had settled, and now the derelict farm was emerging like a butterfly from its battered cocoon.

Driving under the rusted arched sign that read "Runaway Far," Kinney smiled. Hannah had decided not to replace the missing "m" because the name reflected what she'd done: "run away far" from her lonely life in the big city.

Greeting them from the porch with a sweeping wave, Hannah seemed to glow with health and happiness. The cliché about pregnant women turned out to be true in this case, although the glow probably had much to do with Nick Springdale, Evie's handsome brother. Today he was working with a crew to fence off new pasture beside the house. Once the farm had gained popularity from Evie's show, more and more animals found their way to safe haven there. Most of them—great and small—were unceremoniously dumped on the property. Hannah kept the ones that Charlie, her farm manager, felt would be a good fit, and found new homes for the others. Thanks to the Rescue Mafia, she was developing a strong network of hobby farms that spanned several states. Two weeks ago, Kinney had joined Hannah to deliver a particularly nasty donkey to a large sheep farm where his aggression could fend off coyotes. Hannah, a recently licensed driver, had insisted on piloting a truck pulling the trailer. Her courage inspired Kinney; if Hannah could face her fears in life, Kinney could, too.

"I can't believe how fast she's turning this place around," Evie said. "There's a constant stream of contractors." She stared around. "Is there some sort of regulation that all construction workers need to be gorgeous?"

Kinney laughed. "Maybe women are wired to appreciate capable guys. Luckily, you have your own capable guy. He may not be able to build barns, but he can deliver calves and lambs."

"You got the wrong veterinarian," Evie said. "Jon specializes in small animals. But if your pregnant hamster needs a hand, he's your man."

"Whiskey would eat that hamster, wouldn't you boy?" Kinney glanced over her shoulder. The big dog took up most of the back seat, but he looked comfortable enough. He'd paced most of the night, keeping her awake, but it seemed like a moving vehicle soothed dogs as well as babies. "I've made an appointment with Jon to see Whiskey. Maybe he'll have some pointers on rehabilitating him."

"I'm sure he will. He's no pro with a hammer but he's a genius in other ways." Evie's sharp eyes softened with love. "You should find your own handsome genius, my friend. James, for example, seems to be one heck of a businessman. He's already secured permits to start building on his lake-front property even while being on the mayor's bad side."

Pulling into a spot in the packed parking area, Kinney glared at her. "Can you please cut the matchmaking—at least while we're here? Hannah might not appreciate your shoving me into her brother's arms."

"Oh, she would. She told me she wants her brother to settle down and be happy." Evie gathered her things, including her video camera. "A dog cop would make the perfect sister-in-law."

"Please. A dog cop is welcome exactly nowhere." Kinney opened the door. "I didn't realize how much of a pariah I'd become in this role. I was so broken up about Kali when I applied that I couldn't think straight."

Hannah ran down the stairs to hug them both, with Prima at her heels. The scrappy little dog threw back her head and hurled out a volley of barks.

"Cut that out, little lady," Hannah said. "You love Evie and Kinney."

"I imagine the noise is about my passenger," Kinney said. "I rescued a dog from a difficult situation last night. So I brought him out here to—"

"Dump him?" Hannah's smile faded. "No, Kinney, I am not adopting your rescue. I've added another llama and two goats this week alone. Besides, Prima wants to be an only dog."

"I'm not dumping the dog on you." Kinney's voice gave

her away. That's exactly what she'd hoped to do. Whiskey would run out all his anxiety in the rolling green fields. Being stuck at home alone while she worked would be hard on a traumatized dog. "I brought him because I heard Cori would be here."

"She's in the barn, telling Charlie how to manage the llamas," Hannah said. "How she knows so much about camelids is beyond me."

"I know everything about everything," someone said behind them. "At least everything that matters."

Kinney turned to see Cori Hogan, a petite powerhouse who looked like Audrey Hepburn in her heyday—if Audrey were in a motorcycle club. She was wearing jeans, a white T-shirt and a biker jacket that was too warm for the late May day. As usual, her hands were covered in black gloves with orange neon middle fingers. They were her trademark, and she displayed them now by planting her hands on her slim hips.

"We all count on that," Kinney said. "Even the black sheep dog cop."

Cori's dark eyes narrowed. "Why are you being so nice? And humble? What are you hiding?"

Kinney gestured to the car. "It's hard to hide an 80-pound German shepherd."

Cori moved swiftly to release Whiskey from the Prius. The big dog jumped out and immediately bared his teeth at Prima, who was jumping in his face. "Leave it," she said, and the dogs deflated instantly. Cori might be prickly with humans, but she was the calm eye of the storm when animals were around. She watched Whiskey sniff around for a minute or two and then turned to Kinney. "This is the reactive dog you seized last night?"

"I didn't seize him." Kinney didn't bother asking Cori

how she knew; she had feelers all over town. "The owner surrendered him because he didn't want to do the hard work of rehabilitating him."

"Most people don't," Cori said, eying the dog critically. "Especially if the dog has bitten someone."

"He didn't bite, exactly. He was going for a garden hoe and caught my arm. It was just a few small punctures."

Cori pinned Kinney with a glance. "Evie sent me the clip. The first step to recovery is admitting your dog's aggressive. Denial helps no one."

"He's not my dog. I can't keep him, Cori. Sheltering an aggressive dog is definitely a fireable offence with the CCD."

Bridget Linsmore had come out of the barn to join them. She was tall, with long sandy-blonde hair. The dog perpetually at her side was also tall and elegant, but his shiny fur was black. Beau held his ground as Whiskey ran toward him, tail erect. The shepherd veered off at the last minute and circled back to Kinney, who grabbed his leash.

Evie filmed the short scene and when the camera panned to Cori, the trainer presented an orange flipping finger to the lens.

"Don't you have a job, Evie?" Cori asked. "Swinging that camera around is going to get you shot one of these days. Figuratively."

"Now that you mention it, I *don't* have a job," Evie said. "But I do have a mission: to get the mayor ousted."

Cori offered a rare smile, revealing perfect teeth. "That's a worthy mission. But Kinney has a real job. She can't be out gallivanting with you and your pet camera all the time."

"Real job?" Kinney asked. "You hate my job. In fact, you wouldn't return my calls for two months after I accepted it."

"Water under the bridge," Cori said. "I've realized how

valuable it is to have someone on the inside. Especially now that Evie got herself fired from the mayor's office."

"Correction," Evie said. "This is the first job I actually quit."

"You say tomato, I say whatever." Cori waved a dismissive glove. "My point is, the mayor is up to something. I can smell it from way out here. And we need Kinney to keep her job long enough to figure out what that something is."

Kinney laughed. "Evie has a lead on what's currently rotting in City Hall. The mayor told her at Easter that several pedigreed pups went missing. But when she followed up with him later, he denied ever saying it."

"He blamed it on my concussion," Evie said. "But weirder still, none of the breeders he mentioned have reported a stolen puppy."

Cori's delicate eyebrows rose like swallows. "Are you sure it wasn't the concussion? No breeder would keep quiet about a stolen puppy. I would most certainly have heard about it."

"I'm sure," Evie said. "At least, sure enough that I want to dig deeper. I think it's a cover-up."

"Huh." For once, Cori was virtually speechless. She hooked her thumbs into the pockets of her jeans and turned to Bridget. They'd led the Rescue Mafia together for so many years that much went unsaid.

Bridget met her eyes and nodded, as if they'd exchanged words. "Let's look into it. For the moment, however, why don't we talk about rehabbing Whiskey?"

The dog was sitting quietly at Kinney's side. "He looks like the bronze German shepherd in Bellington Square, doesn't he?" she said. "So handsome."

"Except he's a Belgian shepherd," Cori said.

"Really? I guess I should have known that. But they're pretty much the same, right?"

"Not to the owner and operator of said dog. The Belgian is the premier working breed in the world, in my not-so-humble opinion. These are the dogs they train to take down criminals. He's a powerful weapon, Kinney."

Swallowing hard, she stroked Whiskey's ears. They were large, pointy and deceptively soft. "I just need to find a place for him until his owner gets back from her music tour."

Cori shook her head. "This dog has issues. Passing him around like a used book is only going to exacerbate his insecurity. He needs stability, and someone who's willing to work hard to correct his aggression."

"I can't take a dog with issues onto the streets of Dorset Hills. What if he bit someone for real next time?"

Cori waved her arms around like a conductor. "Time to face the music, Kinney. This dog did bite you. It wasn't a catastrophic bite, but it was dog teeth on a human arm. Rule number one in rehabbing a dog: accept the problem. You can't fix what you're denying."

Sadness clogged Kinney's throat for a few seconds. "He was a sweet dog when I met him. Such soulful eyes. He reminded me of Kali."

"He's still a sweet dog," Evie said. "He's just got problems. Like all of us."

"Speak for yourself," Cori said. "Well, I've got problems, most of them caused by City Hall."

Bridget came over and touched Kinney's arm. "I know it's daunting. Honestly, if I could take this dog for you, I would. But a dog that's bitten someone needs focus and special care. It's hard to manage for someone with multiple dogs, and most people with the skills for it do have multiple dogs, like Cori and me."

"But I can't do it. I barely got Kali trained properly and she was a retriever—the pleaser breed. Cori said I was soft. How could I manage an aggressive dog?"

"You *were* too soft on Kali," Cori said. "You treated her like a child and that rarely ends well."

"Cori, she needs a pep talk, not a takedown," Evie said. "This all sounds so complicated. That's why I'm still on the fence about adopting Ari's dog, Thurston Howl. And he's already trained."

Hands back on her hips, Cori glared at Evie. "I don't coddle people with pep talks. You know why? The dog pays. And then I end up having to fix other people's mistakes."

Evie raised her camera. "Could you just preach one more time? Use more glove."

Cori treated her to a double serving of flipping fingers before turning back to Kinney. "Kinney, you have access to the best trainer in Dorset Hills—possibly North America. What are you so worried about?"

"That he could bite someone else? That he could end up getting shipped to a neighboring town or even put down? That I could lose my job *and* fail this dog?"

"Oh, ye of little faith. Buck up, little dog cop, and commit to Whiskey. If you don't commit, he'll know it. Belgian shepherds are the Ferrari of dog breeds. They're smart and hardworking. If you put in the time, he'll turn into the best dog you could ever ask for."

"But I don't want one at all." Kinney's voice rose. "He'll only break my heart."

"No man would dare to break your heart," a deep voice said.

Everyone turned to see James Pemberton, Hannah's brother, getting out of his car. His blue eyes were light and radiant, like a Siberian husky's. His dark hair had grown out a bit and he was sporting a hint of stubble. When they first met, he'd looked like an executive—stiff and formal. Now, despite his navy suit, he was softening around the edges. Dog Town was taking hold of him.

She smiled at him. "The potential heartbreaker is a dog."

"You could do better," he said. "I guarantee it."

He turned to the car and opened the rear door. A tan and black Tibetan mastiff jumped down. Rocky was massive, fluffy and dour-looking.

Kinney felt a sudden jerk and Whiskey pulled the leash out of her hand. He covered the few yards to James' car in a few bounds and got into Rocky's face. Whereas Beau and even Prima had simply held their ground, Rocky took issue. Serious issue. He grabbed Whiskey's neck and tossed him to the ground like a stuffed toy. Jumping up, Whiskey tried to return the favor and soon they were nearly 200 pounds of rolling fur.

"Rocky!" James tried to move between them unsuccessfully. Whiskey's leash wrapped around James' legs and his arms pinwheeled as he tried to keep his balance. He lost the battle and fell backwards into the dusty gravel. The dogs kept their show moving, and literally dragged James along like a trussed sheep. His suit jacket rode up and over his head, and pinned his arms. His yell was muffled in fabric.

Cori signaled Bridget and moved in to grab Whiskey's hind legs. Bridget grabbed Rocky's and they backed away from each other, walking the dogs like wheelbarrows. Kinney ran over to James and helped him to his feet. She tried to straighten his jacket and brush off the dirt, but he stopped her. When she glanced up, she saw his hair was nearly white with dust, making his light blue eyes eerie.

"I'm so sorry," she said, backing away. If any more heat surged into her cheeks, her head would explode.

"It's nothing a shower and dry cleaning won't fix," James said, recovering his almost perpetual smile. "But who's this hooligan that attacked my delicate Rocky?"

"Delicate my ass," Cori said. "Tibetan mastiffs are bred to guard. Whiskey might have started the trouble but he wouldn't have ended it."

James shook his head, scattering fine dust molecules into the air. "It wouldn't have come to that. Rocky's never been in a fight before."

"This is the heartbreaker I was talking about," Kinney said. "Meet Whiskey, my new dog."

Cori released Whiskey, grabbed his leash and backed the dog over to Kinney. She pressed the leash into Kinney's hand as if passing the torch. "This is going to be fun," she said. "There is nothing more satisfying in life than helping a troubled dog. Trust me."

"Oh, I trust you," Kinney said. "It's myself I don't trust."

CHAPTER SEVEN

Cliff Whorley looked up from his paperwork and grunted as Kinney walked into his office. The former state trooper's bushy salt-and-pepper mustache and florid face made her shrink a little. When she'd first met Cliff, she'd been willing to stand up to him because Marti Forrester, then-judge of Dog Court, had cherry-picked her for the dog cop job. Now, however, she had no one backing her. What's more, she had an aggressive dog at home that should have been surrendered to Animal Services. It was enough to suck the sass out of anyone. Anyone except Cori Hogan, perhaps.

"Sit down, Butterfield," he said. It seemed like he placed undue emphasis on the "butter" to make her feel soft.

"Morning, sir," she said. "What can I do for you?"

He crossed his arms over his belly. "We haven't had a chat in a while. What's new?"

All the other dog cops had regular one-on-one meetings with Cliff that produced hearty laughter behind closed doors. Kinney only got called in when needed and there had never been a chuckle out of either of them.

"Nothing much, sir. You know I've mostly been taking

the nuisance calls. Maybe you have something bigger for me today?"

"I do, actually." His mustache twitched as if he were supressing a grin. "A dog nipped one of the mayor's neighbors recently and he wants us to issue a fine to the owner."

She kept her eyes down and her voice calm. "Did it break the skin?"

"Luckily, no. Just ripped the woman's sleeve. She was taking a stick out of its mouth."

"Maybe she shouldn't have tried to take a stick out of a strange dog's mouth?" Kinney said, leaning back in the chair. There had to be more to the story. Something was making Cliff simmer with glee.

"There's zero tolerance for a dog nipping *ever*. You know that, Butterfield." He leaned back, too. "Don't you? It's dog cop 101."

His piggy little eyes bored into her and she took a deep breath. Everything depended on her staying cool. Luckily, there was still a block of ice in her chest that she'd built up during her stint as a social worker. Confronting abusive or neglectful parents required nerves of steel.

"Of course, sir. You've got an address for me?"

Cliff pushed a file folder towards her. "The mayor wants this done at the owner's worksite. The dog is always with him."

"In other words, the mayor wants to make an example of him."

"It's not for us to question the mayor's motives, is it?"

Kinney leaned forward and flipped open the folder. On top of a small pile was a photo of a man with a large, gorgeous black-and-tan dog. Her ribs seemed to close in around her heart and the ice melted a bit. "It's James Pemberton, sir. And his dog Rocky."

"Correct. You know James, if I'm not mistaken. We figured it would be easier coming from a friend."

That was a lie. Cliff knew it would be far more embarrassing for James coming from someone he knew. Perhaps Cliff even knew about Whiskey already and was punishing her, too. She wouldn't put it past the City to "have eyes" on Runaway Farm. Any of the handsome construction workers could be taking a bribe to report in on suspicious activities. Technically, the City had no jurisdiction over the farm since the land was transferred to Wolff County. But that wouldn't stop the mayor from suspecting unlawful plots to arise there. And he wouldn't be wrong. It had become the de facto headquarters of the Rescue Mafia now.

"Rocky is a lovely dog, and James is a prominent property owner and developer in Dorset Hills now," Kinney said. "I can understand giving him a warning, but why make a big show of this?" She held up a photo of the slight tear on a woman's coat sleeve. "It could well have been an accident."

Cliff grabbed the folder out of her hand, leaving her with a bleeding paper cut on her index finger. "We need to keep the mayor happy, Butterfield. In fact, our jobs depend on it."

There it was: the implied job threat. He probably didn't even know how much she needed the income. Or maybe he did. It would be easy enough to check her credit.

"Understood, sir." Standing, she leaned on his desk and splayed her hands. "I'll head down to the jobsite right now and take care of this."

"Butterfield, off. Off!"

She shook her hair in front of her face to hide her smile as Cliff tried to blot the blood from her papercut that now spotted his calendar.

"Sorry, sir," she said. "I guess that proves I'm willing to shed a little blood for my job."

KINNEY FOUND her Prius idling by the front doors of the CCD building. Behind the wheel was Wyatt Cobb, the CCD's latest hire as a canine corrections officer. He was just like all the rest: as handsome and plastic as a Ken doll. Kinney was one of only three women on staff in the CCD's complement of 40, and the only female dog cop. The old boys' club had come as a shock after the female-dominated department of social work. She hadn't fit in particularly well there, either, however. The clients were overwhelmed and her co-workers usually were, too. Locking down her emotion was the only way she could survive.

She walked around the car to the driver's side. "What gives, Wyatt?"

"Boss wanted you to have backup, Butterfield," he said, with a perfect, plasticky smile.

"Cool. But you can back me up from the passenger seat. No one drives me around, Cobb. You can monitor my actions even more easily when you don't have to mind the road."

Wyatt shrugged and opened the door. "As you wish, Butterfield."

She winced before climbing inside. The use of surnames hadn't been part of the corporate culture in social work. Here, her feminine name was being used against her. Pulling out of the parking lot, she headed toward town. The CCD was housed in the old legion hall on the outskirts. That didn't stop people from regularly coming out and tagging the building with graffiti or defacing the bronze Bernese mountain dog statue with toilet paper or costumes. New security cameras hadn't stopped the defilement so Cliff was considering spending tax dollars on an overnight guard.

Wyatt kept up a constant stream of chitchat as they

drove, to which she responded with the occasion murmur of agreement.

"I've never worked so hard to make pleasant conversation," he said at last.

She turned to stare at him. "We're on our way to ticket someone and you've been assigned to make sure I do it. Forgive me if that makes small talk challenging, Wyatt."

He held up his hands. "I'm doing my job, Butterfield. Just like you're doing yours."

"Fine," she said. "But small talk isn't in my job description."

Weaving through town, she noticed a big crowd around the new bronze puppy statues outside the community center. City Hall had made the right choice on this one; it was good to know that still happened sometimes.

"So this guy we're targeting has a Tibetan mastiff, right? Isn't that the most expensive breed on the planet? He must have a huge ego."

Kinney pressed her lips together and said nothing.

"I mean seriously, who'd spend 10 grand on a dog? The guy is obviously compensating for something."

She turned and gave him a cold stare. "You do realize this is the brother of one of my good friends?"

Wyatt had the decency to squirm a little. "Actually, no. Chief didn't mention that. Why'd he ask *you* to do this if you're friends?"

Shrugging, she turned right at the St. Bernard statue in front of the hospital and proceeded down to Lake Longmuir. "Who knows?"

The sun was high and warm, bringing dog owners to the boardwalk in droves. It seemed like every breed imaginable was represented in the constant parade. Kinney slowed, noticing how few mixed breeds moved in the crowd. Cori must be right that no one wanted a good old-fashioned mutt anymore. That said, she'd owned a golden retriever and now a Belgian shepherd. She was living in a glass house, but it was still a shame because many of the mutts ended up getting "exported" to neighboring cities.

Pulling into the parking lot beside the construction site, she turned off the ignition and took a deep breath. She needed to make this as discreet as possible for James. Issuing a fine in front of his staff—and the many pedestrians trailing by—wasn't right and it wasn't fair. The best she could do was pull him aside and keep it quiet.

She got out of the car and didn't bother waiting for Wyatt. He caught up with her anyway, continuing his running commentary.

"Wow, that is going to be one heck of a condo. Is James Pemberton the architect?"

"He's the owner," she said.

"Ah, that explains the fancy dog, I guess. He's loaded."

She turned and gave him a look. "Wyatt, could I ask a big favor?"

"Sure." He was as eager as a beagle working for a treat. "Name it."

"Can you distract people and hold them back so that I can talk to James in private? I don't want to call him out in front of his staff."

"Gotcha. Yeah. Is that him?" He pointed to James, who was standing in a group of men, with Rocky beside him. "He looks like a billionaire. Lucky sonofa—"

"Quiet. Low key, right?"

Wyatt pointed to James, whose arm was up and waving. "Look at that billion-dollar smile," he said. Then something dawned on him. "Butterfield, this guy has the hots for you, doesn't he? Ticketing him is gonna savage his pride. You might as well cut off his—"

"Wyatt! I swear I'm going to toss you into that huge hole if you don't shut up. And don't think I can't do it."

James came over, with Rocky wandering behind him, unleashed. "Kinney, hi! Did you come down to check out my new site?" He looked from her to Wyatt and back. "What's with the uniforms? You guys on a lunch break?"

She gave Wyatt a little shove and he walked over to the group of men James had left. "Is there somewhere we could speak privately, James?"

He gestured to the trailer off to one side of the construction site. "Sure, let's go inside. I'll make you a coffee."

Snapping his fingers, he signaled Rocky to follow. The big dog hesitated, as if to make it perfectly clear he made his own decisions, then moved ahead of them. He had a confident walk, like a burly weightlifter.

Kinney's heart sank as James guided her across the lot with one hand lightly touching her shoulder. She liked him. It was hard *not* to like James. Where Hannah tended to be shy and quiet, her brother was perpetually upbeat. He'd had a lot of good fortune in his life, but he'd also seen his parents split and his mother die too young. He'd clashed so much with his father in the family business that he'd finally left. These events hadn't gotten him down permanently. Maybe he'd come into the world wired for happy, unlike her. Every day she got up anxious and went to bed anxious. In between she worked flat out to hide it. She was pretty sure she succeeded, but it felt like a heavy load sometimes.

James pointed out various features of the worksite as they picked their way through dirt, gravel and bits of asphalt. Most of his words passed right over her head, but she enjoyed hearing his voice. It was deep and oddly calming. If he hadn't been a billionaire businessman, he could have made it on radio.

He didn't so much as acknowledge the episode the day before, where her dog had trussed him up in a leash and dragged him. It was gallant of him, and made her task even harder.

When they reached the trailer, he opened the door. "Welcome to my office on wheels."

She stepped up ahead of James, but Rocky jostled on the stairs to get inside first. A sudden commotion beside the trailer triggered a deep rumble in the dog's chest that Kinney could actually feel. There was a scrabble of feet on asphalt and someone leapt out, and then screamed. Kinney turned quickly—too quickly—and lost her balance. She tumbled sideways down the stairs.

James got his arms out just in time to break her fall. He caught her, spun slightly and placed her on her feet. She tried to get her footing and he steadied her with one arm. Meanwhile, Rocky took the stairs at a bound and charged the person beside the trailer. She had never heard a more menacing bark in her life.

"Rocky, leave it," James bellowed, running after the dog who'd chased the person around the trailer.

Kinney followed and they all circled the trailer to the front again. The young woman with the camera was shrieking. Now Wyatt and the workers were heading for them at a run.

James grabbed Rocky's collar and pulled him backwards. Meanwhile, Kinney signalled Wyatt to hold everyone back. Then she turned on the girl. "Stop that screaming right now. You're agitating the dog. What are you doing creeping around with a camera anyway?"

The girl looked barely out of school, with long caramel

hair, heavy eyeliner and false eyelashes that seemed too heavy to hold up. She straightened her slim shoulders and offered a fake smile. "I'm Madison Parker," she said. "I'm the new documentarian for the City."

"Documentarian?" Kinney asked, advancing on her. "What on earth is that?"

"The mayor asked me to capture some of the cool events going on around Dorset Hills. For posterity, you know?"

Her voice had that lilting uptick so many girls adopted these days. As if it weren't hard enough to be taken seriously in the world. But that was her cynicism talking.

James had crouched to hold Rocky. "What cool event did you expect to capture trespassing on my construction site? This isn't exactly newsworthy."

"It sort of is," Madison said, raising her camera. "The dog cops are here to ticket you because of your aggressive dog." She fanned her flushed face with one hand. "He sure is aggressive. Listen to the growling."

James looked up at Kinney from his crouched position. "Is that why you're here?"

Swallowing hard, she nodded. "I'm sorry, James. Apparently Rocky nipped a woman's sleeve and the mayor heard about it. Since dog court disbanded, the CCD issues fines for dog infractions."

She pulled the extra leash out of her bag that she always carried, and offered it to him. He quickly hooked up Rocky and straightened. For once, his smile was gone and his blue eyes had clouded with anger.

"That was hardly aggression," he said, examining the photo she offered. "That woman took Rocky's chew toy right out of his mouth. She said it was unsafe for dogs and he disagreed."

Kinney gestured to Madison and put a finger to her lips.

"I completely understand how Rocky would take that the wrong way," she whispered. "But there are rules in Dorset Hills about dog nipping. Unfortunately, I do have to issue a fine and request you keep Rocky on leash at all times. For his own safety, and the safety of others."

"Really?" James' eyes narrowed to icy slits. "You're telling me to keep *my* dog on leash for public safety?"

She stared down at the dog. James was calling her a hypocrite because of Whiskey's behavior the day before. And because he was a gentleman, he wasn't doing it on the record for Madison Parker.

"I'm sorry, James," she said. "I didn't want to do this. It's only a hundred bucks."

He shook his head as she pulled out the device that issued tickets. "It's not about the money. Obviously."

The ticket slid out like a yellow tongue that was vaguely obscene. Madison came forward to get a close up and then lunged back when Rocky ripped off another deep bark.

James accepted the ticket. "Thanks for coming out, Kinney. Lovely to see you."

He turned and hauled Rocky into the trailer and slammed the door. Wyatt followed Kinney back to the Prius. She got into the driver's seat and made Wyatt run after the rolling car.

Once settled in the passenger seat, Wyatt laughed. "Guess that means he won't be offering a huge rock anytime soon, Butterfield."

She whacked him with the ticketing device as she backed out of the lot. "Dog cop 101, Wyatt: know when to shut up."

CHAPTER EIGHT

Cliff's mustache seemed bigger and bristlier, although it was only a few hours since she'd sat across from it. Drama and controversy probably made it grow.

He sat in silence, trying to get her to break the silence with babble, but she was too well versed in interrogation techniques to take the bait. So the quiet dragged on, and his mustache twitched more and more. She couldn't take her eyes off it.

Cliff broke first. "That was an embarrassment to the department, Butterfield."

"What was, sir? I went to the site and issued the ticket, just as you asked."

"You lost control of the situation. The dog in question should have been leashed the second you saw he wasn't. Then the aggressive dog you were there to fine ended up practically attacking someone else. We cannot have that kind of escalation in Dorset Hills. It could be mayhem."

"You sent a so-called documentarian to leap out and startle the dog, Chief. Most dogs would take issue with that. It was like you were creating drama to catch it on film."

"I did no such thing. If the mayor wants to document daily life in Dorset Hills, that's his prerogative." He picked up a pen and twirled it deftly on his fingertips. "As I recall, your friend Evelyn Springdale does exactly the same thing for her little show. Perhaps the mayor wants to set the record straight by telling his side of the story."

"Evie's not the mayor. Does it really make sense for the city leader to be creating drama about dogs—the very thing that draws people to Dorset Hills? Good dogs are part of our branding, like you always say. How does filming a dog potentially misbehaving support that brand?"

"I'm not here to debate politics with you, Butterfield." Cliff spun the pen to his other hand, proving his dexterity. "The mayor may work in mysterious ways, but our duty to uphold the law is not mysterious at all."

"I issued the ticket, just like you asked. I did my job."

He stopped spinning the pen long enough to turn his computer monitor to face her. On the screen was a still shot of her in James Pemberton's arms. Rocky was a tan and black blur in the background as he pursued Madison Parker.

"This photo is circulating on social media as we speak, Butterfield. Looks like you got a little distracted on the job." He smirked. "I can understand wanting to leap into the arms of a billionaire bachelor when you should be doing your duty, but you'll need to learn to quell your urges."

The fire flaming up from her stomach threatened to set her hair alight. She stared down at his calendar, still marked with her bloody fingerprints, before answering. "I'm sure you know that I was knocked off balance when Madison Parker leapt out at us."

"Knocked off balance by the unleashed dog, or the charming billionaire?"

Even her lips felt scorching hot. "I'm not in the habit of

falling into the arms of people we're investigating, billionaires or otherwise."

"But you *have* given in to your urges before, Butterfield. Two nights ago, for example."

Her rage transformed instantly into fear, tinged with shame. He knew about Whiskey. But how much did he know?

"What do you mean, sir?" It took a gargantuan effort to keep her voice level. "Are you speaking of Myrtle McCabe? I certainly did have urges around her. More violent than romantic, I suppose. I'm sure you saw my report that she's been firing off canned air to keep neighborhood dogs in line. She's part of an old-guard neighborhood brigade called the Pooch Patrol."

Cliff clicked his mouse a few times and brought up several other images: Kinney with blood on her arm; Kinney and Evie lying in the grass with binoculars; and most damning, Kinney leaving the house with Whiskey on the end of a leash. She swallowed what felt like a gritty lump of sawdust. He knew everything.

"Show me your arm, Butterfield."

She considered getting up and walking out, but that wouldn't end her troubles. Even if she lost her job, Cliff would come after Whiskey and either banish or euthanize him. She stood a better chance of saving him if she stayed the course.

Pulling up her sleeve, she said, "He grazed me by accident in the dusk. I think his mouth happened to be open and collided with my arm."

Cliff shook his head, making his mustache quiver. "A bite's a bite. You won't get far by denying it."

For the first time, Kinney smiled. "Cori Hogan said the same thing."

He rolled his eyes. "Do not liken me in any way to that radical. Let's stick to the subject. You were bitten on the job by an aggressive dog. Yet I don't see that anywhere in your report. Moreover, I see you leaving the Barber house with said dog, but there's no record of it being surrendered to Animal Services. Where is the dog now, Butterfield?"

All kinds of lies and evasions popped into her mind, but she simply said, "At my house."

Cliff raised eyebrows as bushy as his mustache but much darker. "You're harboring a fugitive? The dog's a public hazard. Not turning him in is a fireable offence."

She looked down at her nails, dirty and cracked from field work. "I know, sir. I couldn't turn him in because of Marti Forrester."

This time it was Cliff's face that flamed up. Marti, the disgraced judge, had gotten the top job at the CCD over him. He only had his job now because she quit and left town. She was his Achilles heel, and mentioning her now could be tossing a match into a powder keg.

He tried to spin his pen, fumbled and dropped it. "Explain."

She handed the pen back and he shook his head.

"Marti was with me when I visited this dog in his previous home. She helped me defuse a situation with his owner and we were both so happy and proud when we left. The dog was as calm and devoted as any I'd seen. Months later I find Whiskey is with the owner's sister and her... unpleasant... husband. He's being traumatized by a neighbor who has an issue with both the neighbor and the City. The dog is completely innocent. And now, that stable, wonderful dog is an anxious mess." She picked up Cliff's pen, tried spinning it and failed. It fell on the desk with a clatter. "Marti gave me this job. She trusted me to look out for troubled animals. And she wouldn't want me to surrender Whiskey and traumatize him further. This is a good dog that's been harmed by bad policies. It's not fair to send him away, where he could possibly be euthanized."

Cliff picked up the pen and spun it again. This time it whirled atop his fingertips. "Marti Forrester aside, I agree with you."

She looked up at him, startled. "You do?"

"Of course. It breaks my heart every time we need to ban a dog from Dorset Hills."

"It does?" She hadn't believed he even had a heart, although he clearly was fond of his own perfectly behaved golden retriever.

"Yes, indeed. That's why I'm happy to report that the mayor's taking a new stance on problem dogs. We had a meeting about it today, while you were out flirting with the billionaire." He shook his head. "Is it any wonder why I question putting ladies in the dog officer role?"

She bit her lip. Protesting would only delay hearing about the mayor's new position. "Please tell me about the mayor's change of heart."

He spun the pen from one hand to the other, fully back on his game. "Mayor Bradshaw is the consummate dog lover, just like me. It's given him many sleepless nights to take harsh action against bad dogs. So he's decided to pursue a kinder, gentler Dog Town image. During our pilot test, we'll stop sending dogs away. Instead, we'll rehabilitate them—with appropriate controls and supervision."

Her hand went to her heart. "That's wonderful news. It means I can retrain Whiskey and make him the dog he was when I met him."

"Absolutely. And with the City's blessing, no less."

"Sir, I'm so happy. Thank you. I really value this job and

appreciate being part of this new movement to do more for troubled dogs."

"I'm glad you feel that way, Butterfield. Because you're going to be the one to set a good example for everyone in Dorset Hills who struggles with a bad dog."

Her hand gripped the edge of his desk. "How so?"

"The mayor is launching the Miracle Makeover Dog Training Program. You and your aggressive shepherd will participate and be filmed for the City's documentary."

"Technically the dog isn't mine, sir. He belongs to Jacinda Allen, who'll want to reclaim him when she comes home."

"Actually, no. The dog belongs to the City because he was surrendered. But I've released him into your custody with the mayor's approval because of this show. Whiskey is *your* dog now. Your responsibility. It's official."

Her tongue felt oddly huge and cumbersome in her mouth. "Oh. Well I don't like the idea of this show at all. How does it serve the City to see a dog cop struggling with a troubled dog? It might make them doubt our capacity at the CCD."

"Butterfield, don't overthink this. I have no doubt in the world that you will work wonders on Whiskey and it will raise public confidence about the potential of training dogs well. You'll have a rare opportunity to show people what this fine City is all about. By Independence Day, you'll be able to demonstrate your success to the world."

"The Fourth of July is barely six weeks away, sir."

"It's called the Miracle Makeover Dog Training Program for good reason. Apparently it works wonders in a short time. So you'll be showing off your new skills at the citywide event. The mayor wants fireworks this year."

"Fireworks! Dogs hate fireworks. And Whiskey is noise phobic now."

"He won't be by then. You've got six weeks to turn that dog around."

"That's a full-time job, and then some. I don't see how I can do it so quickly. I've been picking up extra shifts all year."

Cliff gave up spinning the pen and tapped it, instead. "You raise a good point. I think you've been working too hard and it's affecting your judgement. So I've decided to reassign you for now. You need to put your full attention into retraining your dog."

The drumming pen got louder, or maybe it was her heart pounding in her ears. "Reassign me? To what?"

"Well, you know Elsa's retiring this week, and her position will be vacant."

"Elsa? She's our receptionist. That's not just a demotion but a punishment, sir."

"Don't be silly. You're getting hung up on titles." He couldn't even hide the grin hiding under his mustache. "Elsa has a very important role. She's the face of the CCD. She monitors the Tattletail hotline and handles all complaint calls. I've seen the poor lady in tears, sometimes."

She took a deep breath and decided to try another tactic. "I really appreciate that you want to give me time to focus on Whiskey. That's so kind of you. But it sounds like manning the phones might be more stressful than my current role. Let's keep things as they are, sir."

He slammed the pen to the desk with one beefy hand. "Butterfield, I'll stop beating around the bush. It's all been decided. You'll be the poster gal for the Miracle Makeover Program. In the meantime, you'll work reception. If all goes well on the Fourth of July you can keep your job."

She leaned forward, trying to meet his piggy eyes and

failing, because they were darting around the room. "Just to be sure I understand... You're saying if I don't get my traumatized, noise-sensitive dog ready for fireworks on the fourth you'll make an example of me in a documentary?"

He shook his head. "You women get so emotional. See it as an opportunity to educate the public. Show people that they have the power to reform their dogs... and keep them."

Ah. So if she didn't comply with this stupid plan, she'd lose Whiskey, too. They were counting on her to fail and be an example of why draconian policies around problem dogs were necessary.

She stood up, leaned over the desk and slapped it with both hands.

The impact opened her paper cut again and she added streaks of blood to his desk blotter.

"You know what? This all sounds like fun, Cliff." She turned and walked to the door. "Game on."

CHAPTER NINE

"Can you believe they're actually calling this the Miracle Makeover Dog Training Program?" Kinney said, heading into town with Evie in the passenger seat.

"I can believe any crap the City throws out these days. The more outrageous the better, it seems. If it didn't affect my friends and me, I'd laugh my butt off." She looked over at Kinney. "Are you sure you're not going to get into trouble for bringing me along?"

"Oh, probably. But I've already been demoted, set up for public humiliation and threatened with firing. Getting chastised for bringing a friend for moral support can't cause much more damage."

"I guess you're right about that." She leaned back in her seat and smiled. "You're taking this well, all things considered."

"I just remind myself that I've seen and experienced worse. When I was in social services, families were torn apart by domestic violence. It was heartbreaking, especially for the children. So I guess manning the Tattletail hotline and taking dog training isn't so bad." She turned to glance at Evie. "But with Madison Parker, Dog Town documentarian, on the job, I want my own camera crew."

Evie sniffed. "I'll show that upstart a thing or two. Mark my words."

Slowing at City Hall, Kinney admired the German shepherd in Bellington Square. The statue used to remind her of the wolf in Little Red Riding Hood. Now it conjured up Whiskey, who was sitting in much the same pose in the back seat. It still stirred up a bit of fear, but now it was mixed with fondness. The real dog was a sweetheart, if you managed to forget that he was capable of turning on a dime.

The email from City Hall had been fairly cryptic. The first meeting of the Miracle Makeover Dog Training Program was to be held at Pine Grove Alliance Church, one of the oldest churches in Dorset Hills and arguably the quaintest. As they turned and headed for the rolling hills, the white steeple was visible in the distance.

"Do you think they picked a church for optics?" Kinney asked.

"Of course. None of this happens by accident," Evie said, polishing her camera lens. "Every week, people will get to see bad dogs being redeemed redeemed in the perfect setting. I have no doubt Mayor Bradshaw will show up for a photo op at some point"

"Oh no! Do you think he'll be here today?"

Evie shook her head. "Too soon. There's a chance one of the dogs will go for him. He'll wait a few weeks till there's progress. But not too long, in case there isn't progress. At least, that's what I'd tell him to do." She looked up from her lens with a smile. "Thank goodness I'm on the right side of politics now."

Pulling into the church parking lot, Kinney took a deep breath and turned to Whiskey. "Don't embarrass me, pal, okay? That's all I'm asking. I'll work my butt off to help you heal, but I could really do without more media coverage."

Evie laughed. "I, for one, loved seeing that photo of you in James' arms in the *Dorset Hills Expositor* yesterday. It's exactly how I imagined seeing you two. Minus the terror."

"I wasn't terrified."

"James was. He didn't know whether to drop you or go after Rocky and risk someone getting bitten. It's not easy being gallant when you have an aggressive dog."

"Well, it was awful, all of it. I plan to avoid him for a very long time."

They got out of the car and Kinney released Whiskey, keeping a tight grip on his leash. Signs with arrows led them around the side of building.

"You don't even get to go in the front door," Evie said, laughing. "Maybe after the Fourth of July you can pose on the steps. Once your dogs are reborn."

"Time to put a lid on your witticisms," Kinney said. "I've got to look like I'm taking this seriously. I'm the poster child for the program and I'm quite sure the trainer will send a report to Cliff after every class."

"Got it. Taking it seriously. As of... now." Evie pretended to zip her lips.

Opening the door of the basement, Kinney entered a large recreation room. Half a dozen people with dogs of various shapes and sizes had already arrived. At the front of the room, someone was kneeling beside a big box of equipment.

"Is that who I think it is?" Kinney said.

Evie choked back a guffaw. "Well, only one person I know wears gloves with orange fingers in June."

"Did you know about this?" Kinney said, turning quickly. Shaking her head, Evie tried unsuccessfully to smother

her laughter. "Cori kept this top secret. I can't imagine how they enticed her to do it."

Cori stood up and offered a merry wave. Then she worked her way through the crowd and joined them. "Hey, there. I just came over to tell you we're not friends today."

"We're not friends most days," Kinney said.

"True. My friendship is always conditional. But today it's not personal. I've been hired to run this program and I can't give you preferential treatment."

"Why on earth would you accept this job?" Kinney asked. "Your life's work is to embarrass the mayor. And now you're on the payroll?"

"I wouldn't consider those goals to be in conflict," Cori said, grinning. "I'm collecting my paycheck and donating it to worthy rescue causes. That won't keep me up at night. But passing up an opportunity to help troubled dogs and keep the City from banning them? That *would* keep me up at night."

"It's a good point," Evie said. "Plus you're in a position to pick up more information that will help us with our bigger objective of ousting you-know-who."

"Exactly." Cori's dark eyes were never still, monitoring every dog and owner in the room. "We need someone on the inside, now that Kinney is out."

"I am not out. I'm temporarily sidelined because of this dog—the one you urged me to keep, remember?"

Now Cori met her eyes. "I stand by my advice. This dog is going to change you so much you won't want that stupid job anymore. Guaranteed."

"That's putting a lot of weight on one dog's shoulders." Kinney rested her hand on Whiskey's head, but after a polite second or two, he moved away. "See, he doesn't even like me."

Cori rolled her eyes. "I'll get right to work on dispelling

your romantic ideas. You rescued this dog a few days ago. He still doesn't know you from Adam, and quite frankly, you've done nothing to earn his respect yet. The first thing you need to do is drop your arrogance."

"Arrogance! You've got some nerve, Cori Hogan. You are the most arrogant—"

Cori raised her middle finger to her lips. "Shut it, Kinney. Our special guest is here."

In the doorway stood a tall, elegant man with silvery hair and a wide smile showing unnaturally white teeth. He was wearing a slate-grey coat that was too warm for the day but made him look like a movie star of old. Cary Grant, perhaps, or Jimmy Stewart.

Folding her middle fingers, Cori gave him a wave.

Evie followed suit. "I expected him to show up at some point. But if he's officially kicking off the Magical Makeover Program, it must be high profile."

"*Miracle* Makeover," Cori corrected. "There's no magic about it. Just hard work."

Mayor Bradshaw picked his way carefully through the crowd, trying to avoid either unruly dogs, or dog hair.

"Evelyn, how lovely to see you," he said. "You look very well."

"Thank you, sir. I'm really excited to be here to see your new dog program in action. It's a great step forward for the City."

His smile expanded to nearly eclipse the room. "I couldn't agree more, Evelyn. I'm glad there are no hard feelings between us after what happened with Runaway Farm."

"Not at all, sir," Evie said. "Hannah couldn't be happier. The renovation is going well and it's going to make a sweet little inn before too long."

Looking down, he noticed the camera she was trying to hide behind her back. "Evelyn, no. I forbid you to shoot this class for your silly show. I have a real documentarian now." He looked across the room and snapped his fingers at Madison Parker, who was interviewing some of the participants on camera. "She's a professional, you know. Fresh out of film school."

Cori waved her glove in front of the mayor's face. "I'd prefer no cameras at all, Mr. Bradshaw. I don't want to reveal all my trade secrets to other trainers. And from a theatrical standpoint, imagine how much more impact there will be when we can reveal these dogs fully transformed at the Fourth of July festival."

The mayor stared over her head, which wasn't that hard as he was well over a foot taller. "The cameras stay, Miss Hudson. And please... call me 'Mayor.'"

It gave Kinney some comfort to see that he still despised Cori, even though he was using her to advance his agenda. Politics really did make strange bedfellows.

Finally, his eyes turned to Kinney. "I don't believe we've met."

"We have, sir, at a number of events. But I don't expect you to remember everyone. I'm Kinney Butterfield."

"Ah yes, the dog officer with the gentleman." He gave a little smile. "That photo went viral, I hear."

Kinney's face flushed as she pressed her lips together. She stared down at Whiskey, trying to regain her composure. When she looked up again, Madison's camera was zooming in. She whispered to Evie, "This day could not get any worse."

Evie looked over her shoulder, and whispered back, "Challenging fate that way ends up biting you in the butt, I'm afraid."

Turning quickly, Kinney saw two more participants in the doorway: James Pemberton and Rocky.

"Oh, no," she said, and then clapped her hand over her mouth.

"Oh, yes," the mayor said. "After that shameful display at his worksite, it made sense to sentence Mr. Pemberton and his dog to mandatory reform class."

Cori's shout for attention prevented him from saying more. She'd moved to the front of the room. "We're all here, so let's get started, people. I can't wait to see you transform your relationships with your dogs through my Miracle Makeover Program. Let's get started with a fun little exercise so I can see how you handle your dogs. Form a circle facing forward, with dogs on the inside. Spectators, take your seats at the side of the room."

Kinney moved into the circle and positioned Whiskey to her left. Her heart was thundering as if this were a life-and-death situation. With the mayor, Cori, James, and Madison's camera observing her performance, that was pretty much how it felt. This dog was unpredictable, and she was a dog cop—someone who was supposed to know how to deal with all challenges related to dogs. It felt like her whole identity was on the line.

"Relax," a voice said behind her.

She glanced over her shoulder. James looked cool and collected, although his wide white smile was only half as bright as usual. "How can I relax? I'm going to make a fool out of myself."

"What's the worst that can happen?" he said.

Now she turned right around. "James, they could take our dogs away from us. And in my case, I could lose my job." She rolled her eyes. "What's left of it. I've already been demoted over adopting Whiskey."

His blue eyes widened. "I didn't know. I'm sorry to hear that."

"And I'm sorry about what happened yesterday. I can't believe the coverage that silly incident got."

"Don't worry about it," he said. "The way I look at it is that I needed to knuckle down on Rocky and now I'm locked in with a good trainer. I've been away so much over the past year that his behavior slipped. Getting ticketed and called out in the paper was a wake-up call."

Kinney just stared at him. How could he be so gracious about what had happened? She was seething whereas it rolled off him, like water off a duck's back.

"Thank you," she said. "It's kind of you to let me off the hook."

"Kinney, it might surprise you, but it's not every day a pretty girl falls into my arms. I'll forgive a lot for that."

A prickle of heat rushed through her, leaving her cheeks warm. James must have girls falling all over him all the time. He was handsome, rich and genuinely kind. It was too bad they were wrong for each other. He needed someone graceful and gregarious—a woman of the world. The opposite of her.

"Kinney and James?" Cori called from the front of the room. Madison was shooting over her shoulder. "Time to stop flirting and pay attention. This is a big part of your problem: you need to focus on the dogs. It's always important to focus on your dogs, but when there's trouble with said dogs, you need to drop everything else and make that your top priority. Can you do that?"

Kinney mumbled something under her breath and offered a low flip of her finger to Cori, who grinned instantly in response.

James said, "Of course. I'm ready to put my all into

Rocky."

"Okay, I'm going to play some music and you're going to walk the dogs forward in a circle. When the music stops, you ask the dog to sit."

She hit a key on a boombox and "Another One Bites the Dust" rang out. Kinney shuffled forward with Whiskey, who kept turning to eye Rocky and James. Rocky pranced forward on his leash, flashing some teeth. Soon Whiskey was pulling backwards and Kinney had to hold the leash with both hands. Meanwhile Rocky was tripping James, making him hop awkwardly.

Kinney caught a quick glimpse of the mayor perched on a child's plastic chair, somehow still looking elegant. Evie was slouched in the corner, shooting from behind a mini chalkboard.

The music stopped abruptly and Whiskey danced around like he didn't know the "sit" command, which he totally did. He finally planted his butt, but in reverse, staring at Rocky.

Cori moved through the crowd, took Kinney's arm and moved her ahead in the circle. Now she was between a woman with a reluctant Scottie named Angus, and a tall teenaged girl with a small gold dog named Nugget.

"Just tell him to watch you and then praise him," Cori said. "He needs to pay attention to you at all times, not the other dogs."

The music started again, and without the distraction of Rocky, Whiskey behaved nicely.

Cori did a number of other exercises, including meeting other dogs head on, and walking around obstacles. Whiskey did well through it all, unless Rocky moved too close, which the fluffy instigator kept trying to do. Finally, they formed a single line in front of their leader.

"I've seen enough, thanks. As I suspected, everyone here has the same basic challenge: your dog does not see you as its leader. You're just someone at the end of the leash who may or may not be trustworthy. Given that, you can hardly blame the dog for not listening. It doesn't matter if your dog behaves perfectly at home, by the way. What really counts is how the dog behaves everywhere else. And that's where the relationship comes in. If your dog trusts you, it will listen to you, whether you're standing in the middle of a busy highway, in a park or at a shopping mall. So that's what we are going to work on over the next six weeks: your relationship."

Kinney raised her hand. "But what if a dog has just come into your care? You can't wave a magic wand and get him to trust you."

Cori shrugged. "Building a bond can be quicker than you think. The dog just needs to know you have its back. That doesn't come from nursing it like a baby. It comes from making calm, wise decisions consistently. Basically, you need to be worthy in the dog's eyes of paying attention."

"I don't see how that can happen in barely six weeks," Kinney pressed.

"It can happen for the dog, I guarantee it. Can it happen for you? Are you ready to commit to becoming worthy of this dog's respect?"

The heat rose in Kinney's cheeks once more. When she saw Madison's camera zooming in on her, she turned away.

James raised his hand. "I agree that this program is too short to turn things around, even when you've owned the dog for years. It takes time for bad habits to develop and it takes time to unravel them."

Cori put her hands on her hips. "James, I've watched you and Rocky closely. He thinks you're a pal and a playmate.

But he doesn't think you're someone to look up to and respect."

"Well, I've travelled a lot in the past year. He's been with different caregivers."

"Inconsistency isn't good for a dog, granted," Cori said. "But this is more about you wanting to be the good guy all the time. You're like Rocky's fun little brother instead of his leader."

"That's a bit harsh," he said, still smiling.

"When you have an aggressive dog, you don't need mollycoddling, you need truth. And the truth is you're too worried about being liked to be firm with your dog." Cori grinned at him. "It's actually quite freeing to make your peace with being disliked sometimes."

The mayor sprang up with ease from his miniature chair. "Wonderful, Miss Hudson. This is like therapy and dog training all in one. It's gratifying to be able to provide this to our troubled citizens for free. Where do we go from here?"

Cori circulated with handouts. "Here's the homework assignment. Next class we break into smaller groups and start exercises in the community."

Kinney beat it to the door to avoid further contact with the mayor. Whiskey had other ideas, however. He pulled hard to the left so he could reach Mayor Bradshaw and stuck his long black nose where it didn't belong.

The mayor literally jumped and gave a startled squawk. Kinney almost laughed, despite her embarrassment. Rarely did the mayor show any emotion, at least in public, but getting goosed was too much even for him.

"I'm so sorry, Mayor," she said.

He brushed off his slacks with a look of supreme distaste. "I wish you the best, Miss Butterfield. You certainly have your work cut out for you."

CHAPTER TEN

The phone rang again and Kinney flinched. All morning she'd been sitting at the front desk of the CCD offices fielding Tattletail hotline calls about pressing issues like dogs tipping garbage, peeing on ornate bushes, and chasing neighborhood squirrels. Now she understood why Elsa had taken early retirement. It was difficult to be polite to irate citizens complaining about seemingly small issues. But she took a deep breath and smiled as she reached for the phone. Whatever the cost of redeeming herself and Whiskey, she was ready to pay it.

After recording the details of yet another poop infraction, she turned to see Cliff Whorley coming out of his office looking extra pompous. He clapped his beefy hands for attention and the staff gathered around him. Kinney took off her headset and stood, to look like a team player.

"I've just had an important call from the mayor's office," he said. "The CCD has been named honorary patron of the Fourth of July festival. As you know, this is the biggest civic event except Christmas, and they've trusted it to our hands. We have just over five weeks to pull things together, with the help of the City's recreation committee. I need a crackerjack planner to grab the reins. Volunteers?"

Kinney's hand shot up. "I'll do it."

Cliff's mustache twitched disapprovingly. "Butterfield, I've never even seen you at a department party. What makes you the social butterfly today?"

"Recent events, sir. I guess I've been too focused on my job and need to get more involved with the department." She offered a big, fake smile around the room. "This will give me a chance to get to know everyone better."

He targeted Wyatt Cobb with a pointed stare, but Wyatt looked at the floor. Finally Cliff called, "Anyone else up for it?"

No one raised a hand. The so-called honor of organizing the endless Dorset Hills fetes was lost on most people, including Kinney. But the role would give her an excuse to get away from her desk. One morning tied to the phone was already suffocating her. A desk job had always seemed like a ball and chain. She needed to keep moving.

"Done," Cliff said, still looking disgruntled. "Butterfield, present a business case by end of week. This event needs to be a feather in our cap." He offered what passed for a grin. "No pressure."

Kinney wasted no time in getting another clerk to cover for her and slipping out of the office. In the Prius, she opened the window and sucked in deep breaths, as if her head had been held under water too long. She was never going to make it out of the receptionist role alive.

Pulling up beside the old mansion that housed the Hospital Foundation, she waited till Remi Malone climbed in the car and settled Leo, the most loveable beagle in the world, into her lap. She rarely went anywhere without him. He was her canine shield against the world.

"What's up?" Remi asked. "You said it was urgent."

"It's life or death," Kinney said, grinning. "I just volunteered to organize the Fourth of July festival and you know I could not possibly care less about public gatherings. You, my friend, are the queen of Dog Town fetes."

Remi's hand instantly began stroking Leo's silky ears, a sure sign she was stressed. "That's the biggest event of the year, second to Christmas, Kinney. We only have five weeks."

"You can do this in your sleep," Kinney said. "Heck, Leo could do it in his sleep."

Leo lolled his head back and looked at Kinney upside down. It was impossible to resist those eyes and those ears. She took one hand off the wheel and patted his head.

"Besides," she added, "We have the City crew to back us. You'll just be steering the show with me. Will you help?"

Remi stared at Kinney's profile as she pulled out into noon traffic. "Only if you tell me what this is really about."

Kinney sighed. Remi was getting a lot cagier. When they'd first met, the sweet, shy woman would say yes to almost any good cause, no strings attached. Now, she'd gotten wise from being exploited by the Rescue Mafia, where she typically got most of the grunge work and none of the credit.

"I've been assigned to desk duty," Kinney said. "I need to earn my regular job back and it won't be by manning the phones."

"Organizing the Fourth of July event is going to win you your job back? Is it that important to Chief Whorley?"

They passed the bronze St. Bernard outside the hospital and turned right. "Not exactly. But this role gets me out of the office, where I can find opportunities to do things that actually matter. You know, like saving dogs' lives."

"That's kind of random. It means being in the right place

at the right time." She shifted Leo into full-on baby position. "What else aren't you telling me?"

Glancing at her, Kinney said, "You didn't used to ask so many questions."

"My nerves couldn't take the shock of some of the situations I was pulled into. I love helping a good cause, you know that. I'd just like a decent heads-up."

"Fair enough." She turned again at the Dalmatian outside the fire station. Today the bronze was wearing a helmet. Sometimes it was draped in a firehose. The firefighters tried to keep things light. "So here goes: I got a tip from Evie about a possible cover-up in the mayor's office. I'd like to look into it but it's nearly impossible when I'm tied to a desk nine to five and have Miracle Makeover training classes and homework. I need an excuse to get out and investigate, and I need more hands."

Now they were in Riverdale, one of the most popular neighborhoods in Dorset Hills for the "new guard." The people who'd flooded into the city after it became famous had bought into Dog Town branding hook, line and sinker. Nearly every house was decorated according to the City's rules, with appropriate seasonal decorations. Right now, most people only had tasteful dog sculptures made of twisted brown vines or metal. In just a few weeks, however, the gardens with matching flowers in approved colors would be in full bloom.

"Where are we going?" Remi asked, still not confirming her buy-in. "This doesn't feel like a party planning expedition."

"It is, I promise," Kinney said. "The key is to combine party planning with detective work. We can do this."

Remi finally laughed. "Why am I always getting dragged

into Rescue Mafia work when I can't even get full acceptance into the group?"

"I don't have my gang colors either," Kinney said. "And technically, it's not a Mafia project yet. Cori and Bridget are aware of the situation but I have details they don't." She turned down a side street where properties were larger and the houses older. "Good thing being tied to the front desk doesn't stop me from accessing CCD technology."

"At least tell me the so-called crime before we get to wherever we're going," Remi said.

"The mayor told Evie about some stolen purebred puppies and then denied all knowledge of it later. He blamed it on Evie's concussion, and she had doubts herself. But I found records on our system of cases being opened and closed at the exact time and with the exact breeders Evie mentioned. But when I click on them, access is denied."

"That is weird," Remi said. "Definitely worth poking around." She adjusted Leo's position. "But let me get this straight: your goal is to solve the problem of the missing puppies and win your way back into CCD favor?"

"Exactly."

"Even though the CCD apparently wants the cases closed?"

Kinney waved her fingers dismissively. "Everyone wants the truth exposed, don't they?"

"In Dog Town? Hardly. Seems to me that digging into this problem might just get you demoted into the dumpster. Do you have a death wish?"

"Some have said so, yes. My mom always called me a thrill seeker."

Kinney fell silent as they wove through the twisty streets. Her mom was a helicopter parent before that was even a thing.

Her efforts to micromanage her three kids had produced one dutiful daughter who stayed close to home, married and reproduced early and had dinner with her parents twice a week. The other two kids, Kinney and her brother, had been lifelong rebels. Once she graduated from her psychology studies, she put the continent between her and her hometown of Seattle. Since moving to Dorset Hills, she'd only been home once for Thanksgiving, just to get a reminder of why she'd moved in the first place. Her mother couldn't wrap her head around the concept of Dog Town and lamented how Kinney had "squandered her looks and talent on dogs."

Pushing the memories away, she pulled up in front of a large, old house and put the car in park. "Here's the thing, Remi. Once I know something's rotten, I can't *not* smell the decay. Sometimes I wish I could. So I need to get to the bottom of this, even if it gets me in hotter water." She took the keys out of the ignition and jingled them. "I still want to believe that good triumphs in the end."

Remi sighed and hugged Leo closer. "Me too. So count me in."

"Just follow my lead and play along, okay?" Kinney said, getting out of the car.

"Got it. Can Leo come in?"

"Definitely. He actually has a key role in softening up our source."

They went up the walk and Kinney knocked on the red front door. There was a cacophony of barking behind it, and finally it cracked open a few inches. All Kinney could see was a dark eye, corkscrew curls and a blue and black lumberjacket.

Leann Cosburn cursed and tried to slam the door, but Kinney wedged her steel-toed boot into the opening. "Leann, relax. I'm not here in my dog cop capacity. In fact, I don't have dog cop capacity anymore. I was demoted to reception."

The door opened a few more inches and Leann's skeptical face appeared in full. "Well, that's good news, but I doubt you drove all the way out here to tell me that."

"True. I came with a rather large favor to ask. Although it will actually end up doing you a lot of good, too, if you say yes."

Now the door swung wide open and Kinney could see a pack of hounds held back by a baby gate. That didn't shut off the noise though. They howled when the door opened and escalated when they saw Leo. He turned in Remi's arms with a low whine, and then collapsed in dramatic defeat.

"That's one lazy hound," Leann said, shaking her head. But her hand reached out involuntarily, proving as always that no one could resist Leo.

"Right?" Remi said. "I used to think he had lapdog genes but I had him tested. All beagle."

Leann smiled despite herself. "You're Remi Malone, right? I've seen you and Leo at hospital fundraisers."

Remi nodded. "I'm just out with Kinney today because she's starting to coordinate the Fourth of July festival."

"Man, it seems like we just got through the last one." Leann's arms came out to welcome Leo. "This isn't a typical beagle. I have 15 of them, so I should know."

"He may be the only service beagle in town," Remi said. "I got so lucky when I rescued him."

Kinney cleared her throat. "When you two are finished bonding over hounds, can I get to my favor, Leann?"

Leaning against the doorframe cradling Leo, the dog breeder nodded. "Shoot. But make it fast. I have contractors working out back and I don't trust them not to let a dog escape."

"Like Remi said, it's about the Fourth of July," Kinney began. "My idea for this year's theme is to showcase local dog breeders. We'd give the top breeders a booth so that they could share information with the public."

"I love that idea," Remi said. Her enthusiasm was genuine and contagious. "Of course you'd be the beagle expert, Leann. Everyone knows your hounds are prizewinners."

Leann kept her eyes on Leo. "It's not always good to stand out in Dog Town, in my experience. No attention comes without risk."

"I know what you mean," Kinney said. "I heard you lost a pup six weeks ago."

Leann looked up quickly, eyes wide. "Who said that?"

"Dog cops hear things. You know how it is."

Now Leann stood fully upright and Leo squirmed in her arms, trying to lick her face. As always, he sensed when someone was stressed. "Then I'm sure you know I got the pup back. And I never said another word about it, just like I—"

She stopped abruptly and her face turned a mottled pink.

"It's okay, I understand everything," Kinney said. "Are you going to invite us in? So we can talk more about the Fourth of July?"

Leann's head snapped back and forth and she passed Leo to Remi. "I'm happy to do whatever you need. Just like I always cooperate. But I don't want any more disruptions today."

"No problem," Kinney said. "I'll be in touch with more details about the breeder showcase. Thanks so much for participating, Leann."

The door slammed shut and they went back down the walk.

"Was that weird or what?" Remi asked.

"It was weird all right," Kinney said, once they were seated in the car. "I'm just going to check something. Let me pull ahead a bit and then I'll go back for a quick look."

She parked half a block away and left Remi and Leo in the car. Jogging back, she slipped down between the houses. It was easy enough to climb onto Leann's air conditioner to peek into the backyard. She'd expected fairly major work with all the banging and sawing, but the magnitude of it still took her by surprise. The building in progress looked like a mid-sized indoor kennel. A very tall construction worker with flaming red hair sticking out from his helmet looked up just as she ducked. She'd seen him at Runaway Farm before. Good tradespeople got around, apparently.

Jumping down, she ran back to the car, thinking hard and saying nothing till they'd turned off the street.

"What'd you see?" Remi finally asked.

"Leann's building a kennel out back," Kinney said. "I checked her profile this morning and there were complaints on record about the state of her facility. She'd submitted letters and records attesting to the fact that she wasn't making enough from her breeding program to upgrade as the city requested."

"So she won a lottery?" Remi asked.

"Either that, or someone paid her a hefty price to keep quiet about the stolen pup."

"Ah, so now the plot thickens," Remi said. "And it'll build to fireworks by the fourth, I reckon."

Kinney shrugged and then nodded. "Cover your ears, partner."

CHAPTER ELEVEN

The muffled thud of clapping gloves brought Kinney out of her trance. She was sitting on the dingy tile floor of the church basement stroking Whiskey's ears. He was lying beside her, watching all the other dogs and showing none of the signs of aggression Cori had written on the whiteboard at the front of the room: stiff posture, fixed stare, ears forward, hackles up, tail erect and wagging slowly. Apparently, she needed to learn to read dog and speak dog if she wanted to help Whiskey over his trauma and prevent reactive behavior.

"Kinney, off the floor," Cori said, trying to snap gloved fingers. "Are you this dog's pal or its leader?"

"Can't I be both?" She scrambled to her feet. "I'm trying to build a bond with him."

"That's not how you do it." Cori came over and managed to loom over Kinney despite being six inches shorter. "You don't roll around, snuggle and coo with a dog that doesn't respect you. You stand tall, you exude confidence, and you *never* ask the dog to do you the favor of obeying. You expect obedience just because you're worthy."

"But he barely knows me. How is he going to know I'm worthy?"

Cori rolled her eyes, as if it were the dumbest question she'd ever heard. "How could we work together so long without your knowing this? You've handled plenty of dogs much worse than Whiskey, even at work."

She was right, of course. The difference now was that Kinney cared about Whiskey's good opinion. She didn't want him to obey for the sake of obeying. She wanted him to like and respect her. Maybe that was due to the regal way he carried himself, and the depths of understanding in his eyes. More than any dog she'd ever encountered, he seemed like he had the capacity for the magical bond people mentioned in reverential tones. Cori and Bridget always said that many dogs crossed your path, but few became the dogs of your heart. It would have sounded silly to share this out loud in front of the class, but she was starting to wonder if Whiskey could be that dog for her. She hadn't believed she could love a dog ever again after Kali; maybe she was wrong.

Or maybe Whiskey was clouding her judgment by playing so hard to get. They'd spent a lot of time together over the past few days, and while he tolerated her, he clearly didn't think she was all that. She was very much the one-down in this situation and she wanted to even the score.

Cori poked her with an index finger and made her jump. "Stop ruminating. There's no ruminating in the Miracle Makeover Dog Training Program. We're all about action here."

The rest of the class tittered nervously, as did Madison, the class documentarian, from her vantage point on the side-lines. Cori picked on Kinney more than anyone else, but she wasn't above sharing a few plain truths with others. Now she turned to James, who was standing on the opposite side of the room. Kinney presumed it was to keep their dogs apart, but maybe he was still angry at her despite his kind words. It wasn't something she could do anything about right now but it bothered her just the same.

"Shoulders back, James," she said. "Posture is half the battle with dogs. You need to carry yourself like a leader, not like a comrade." She stared around the room. "If you still prefer being liked to respected, kick that notion to the curb right now. I can tell you from vast experience that it is far preferable to be respected—by either dogs or humans. Farm animals, too, if you must know."

Brianne, the gawky teenager with lanky blonde hair, raised her hand. "Sorry, ma'am, but I still don't quite understand how we do that. Nugget barely acknowledges me."

Cori walked over to Nugget, who was draped across Brianne's big sneakers. "Off," she said. When the dog didn't move, she nudged him gently with her foot and he leapt away as if she'd zapped him with a taser. Leaning toward him slightly, she got into the small dog's space. Nugget responded by planting his butt and giving her his full attention. "That's how you do it, Brianne. Feel your inner leader and project it calmly." She walked off, saying, "And never let your dog sit on your feet. Or the couch, or the bed for that matter. Four on the floor."

Standing in front of Jenny Kent, a polished and popular hair stylist, she looked down at Angus, the Scottish terrier. "Honestly, Jenny, you've got the biggest challenge in this room. Angus is 100 percent full of himself and most of that is wired into him. Terriers are bred to hunt and kill and are mostly indifferent to polite society. They're stubborn little cusses, and I love them for that, but you've really got to find your backbone if you want him to respect you."

Jenny's eyes welled up with tears. "But how? You know I

just got him back after being banished from Dorset Hills for eating the school rat." She looked around at Brianne's horrified gasp. "I mean, he shook it to death. He didn't eat it."

Cori gave Brianne a withering look. "I don't permit gasping in this room over dog behavior. You know why?" Brianne shook her head meekly. "Because dogs are animals. Sometimes they do what they're bred to do and that's that. Our jobs as their leaders is to provide direction against their instincts, and to remove opportunity."

"I need to figure out how to keep Angus." Jenny was full-on crying now. "He barely listened to me before but now that he's back, it's like I'm no better than a handmaid carrying his poop."

Cori laughed. "That sounds about right for a Scottie. But believe it or not, you can get out in front of this dog if you follow my advice. I can tell you're highly motivated, Jenny. You just need to transform yourself into a leader in six weeks."

Now Kinney laughed and Cori turned on her. "What's so funny?"

"You think it's easy to transform into a dog leader in six weeks—five weeks, now—but come on... you're *you*. There's no one else like you in Dorset Hills. You've got to dumb this down for us. Like, 'Dog Leadership Made Easy for Newbies.'"

Closing her eyes for a second, Cori took a few breaths. Then she opened them and clapped her gloved hands again. "Okay. I'll put a detailed list together. Normally I don't coddle my students like this but there's a hard deadline. I want all of you to be able to keep your dogs, so if I have to spoon-feed you, I will." Turning, she looked straight into Madison's camera lens. "Also, I really want to stick it to the City. To do that, I need all of you to succeed."

James raised a tentative hand. "Are you saying the City will seize our dogs if we can't master this?"

Cori shrugged. "As brilliant as I am, I can never guess what the City is going to do next. All I can say is that they promised they won't meddle with obedient dogs who pass my quality assurance exam. On the Fourth of July, I'll put you through your paces at the festival. Let's just assume everyone will pass, because my Miracle Makeover Program cannot fail." She shook her finger. "I will move into your homes if I need to and make sure you're following the rules."

Brianne seemed to shrink about a foot at the very thought and moved closer to Nugget.

"She's joking, Brianne," Kinney said.

"Not joking," Cori said. "I have a sleeping bag in my truck and I'm not afraid to use it. Now, down to business. You're going to pair up and do an exercise. Everyone here drives, so I want you to head to Clover Park, which most Dog Towners avoid because it's still awaiting its City facelift." She turned to a large cardboard box and opened it. "Here are your goodie bags. Your mission today is to figure out what really motivates your dog. Is it food? Is it toys? Is it praise? Is it free time to run? Every dog is different, but if you figure out how to turn its crank, you can get its attention. Then you can worry about impressing your dog." She picked up the first two bags. "Kinney and James, you're accountability buddies. I've listed some exercises, and I want you to film each other doing them."

"But our dogs hate each other," Kinney said. "You're setting us up to fail."

Cori shoved the goodie bag into her hands. "You keep missing the point, Kinney. If you fail, I fail. And I never fail. The fact that Whiskey and Rocky don't get along is exactly why you're paired up. It's the perfect situation to bring about change." She walked over and handed a bag to James. "And since you're both oblivious, the reason your dogs don't get along is because they're picking up on your tension."

"What tension?" James said. "You already said I'm too relaxed. You can't have it both ways."

Cori rolled her eyes. "Of course I can. It's my program. I said I'd spoon-feed you on some things, but this one you can figure out yourself. You're a big boy, James."

Kinney came over, keeping Whiskey on the opposite side, and tugged James' arm. "Let's go. Don't give her more ammo, James."

"Tell me she's that good," he muttered, following Kinney out the side door. "Because it's the first time I've ever wanted to slap a woman."

"She is that good," Kinney said. "I've put my life in her hands without hesitation during risky rescue situations. So, let's just trust the process."

He gave a reluctant nod. "I'll meet you there. I may trust the process but I don't trust the dogs in the same car."

———

MADISON PARKER WAS ALREADY WAITING beside her quirky red cube-shaped car at Clover Park when Kinney arrived. She was wearing a hoodie and sweats, making her look even younger, but her alert gaze and stiff posture reminded Kinney of the warning signs of aggression Cori had listed earlier. She was apparently determined to do whatever it took to get some good footage for her documentary. Kinney suspected she had little interest Brianne, Jenny or the two men in the class with bull terrier mixes.

James pulled into the lot in a cute little convertible with the top down. Rocky lounged in the back as if he didn't like his fluff ruffled. The balmy breeze promised summer soon, and daylight now stretched till close to nine.

They walked deep into the park, hoping to shake Madison and failing, as expected. At least she kept far enough back that they could almost pretend she wasn't there.

Kinney set to work with Whiskey. She'd expected his biggest motivation to be food; he had a healthy appetite and loved liver treats. When she pulled items out of the goodie bag and worked through Cori's exercises with him, however, she got to explore what really inspired him. He seemed indifferent to praise, but his eyes lit up over the squeaky toy and the chew stick. When she finally pulled out the tennis ball and hurled it across the field, he literally sprang to life. Racing across the field, he came directly back and dropped it at her feet. Following Cori's written orders, she put him through some drills and made fetch the reward. At the end, he sat with his tongue lolling out the side of his mouth. It was the first doggy grin she'd ever seen on his face.

"Wow," she said, turning to James, who was filming her with his phone. "That just goes to show how little I know this dog."

"My turn," he said. "I don't think Rocky gives a crap about any of those things, to be honest. Maybe he completely lacks motivation."

True to his breed, Rocky was a still-waters-run-deep kind of dog. He was deceptively placid, barely changing expression. Most of the time, like now, he preferred to be in regal repose. But behind that benign demeanor was a serious guard dog. As Cori had kindly pointed out, Rocky just wasn't sure exactly what he was guarding and therefore misfired sometimes.

The dog knew his commands well but he went through them reluctantly and in slow motion. James asked him to sit and he pondered for a second or two before obeying. Then James offered the squeaky toy and Rocky literally looked away. Squeakers were clearly beneath him. Praise made him turn the other cheek. And the tennis ball... well, it just rolled down the slight incline. After a couple of seconds, Rocky got up, ambled forward and lifted his leg on it.

Kinney laughed so hard she could hardly hold the phone steady.

"Stop laughing, this is tragic," James said, although he was smiling himself. "You heard Cori. Motivating my dog is the first step toward connecting with him. If we can't connect, he'll never accept me as his personal deity."

Still laughing, Kinney said, "Cori didn't put it quite that way. Now, try the treats kit. There's a bonus pack in case the liver didn't work."

James followed Rocky and told him to sit again. This time he offered tiny scraps of items from a day-of-the-week pill container. Rocky turned his head one way, and then the other, refusing to accept a single morsel. Every bit James tossed down, Rocky ignored and Whiskey hoovered up.

"At least Rocky's not growling," Kinney said. "Neither dog has an issue with food guarding. That's something."

"Yeah, but yours likes fetch and mine likes... nothing."

"He's just picky. Nothing wrong with discriminating taste. There are more treats when this batch is done."

James plucked a small square of food from the last container and suddenly, Rocky's big head swivelled. He looked up with bright eyes, and a long string of drool trailed out of his mouth.

"Oh my goodness, he's alive," Kinney said.

James gave her a look as he let Rocky take the treat. He flipped the container and read the writing on the bottom. "Tripe. Oh man, it stinks like you wouldn't believe."

After putting Rocky through a few more commands, he let him lick the tripe residue from the container, and then tried to wipe the smell off his hands on the grass.

Kinney picked up Cori's list, and said, "What's next?"

"Hide and seek? Well, this oughta be interesting," he said. "What if one of the dogs takes off?"

"Cori told me to let Whiskey off leash in parks if there's no one around," Kinney said. "She assured me he won't take off. Apparently dogs like to dance with the ones who brung them, even if they don't respect them very much."

James led her further into the park, where there was a little playground, now empty. It was early evening, and still quite bright, but the park was too lackluster to bother for most families, even on weekends. It wouldn't be long till the City planted a few big bronzes to bring in the crowds. Recently, they'd started offering cheap dog paraphernalia to anyone who had photos with each and every bronze dog in the city. The treasure hunt had become a big draw.

"This is far enough," Kinney said, peering around. "It looks like we lost Madison somewhere. Bonus!"

James reached over and tapped her shoulder. "You're it."

He took off into the trees and she followed, laughing. He was much faster than she was, and agile to boot. But she had something he didn't: Whiskey. Bred for herding, the dog wove around James' feet, pushing him gently away until he came to a stream. When James had nowhere else to go, Kinney raced up, punched him in the arm and yelled, "Tag."

Again Whiskey worked in her favor. He ran back and forth between them, cutting James off and slowing him down. Meanwhile Rocky just ambled along, looking disgusted.

Kinney ran back to the playground and Whiskey did his thing, herding James further and further away. "How did you get him to do that?" he yelled. "Did Cori brief him in advance?"

"No idea. He's just some kind of genius I guess."

While the dog kept James at bay, she climbed up on the slide and sat there, grinning. Finally James pulled the last of the liver treats out of his pocket and threw them on the ground. Whiskey took the bait, literally. James ran over to the slide and scaled the steps. "You're in trouble, lady."

Just as he reached the top, she pushed off. It was a tall slide, the old-fashioned fun kind that was now deemed unsafe for kids or City Hall's legal department. She felt the familiar whoosh as she sailed down, and smiled as her hair flew back. For just a second, all her worries about work, Whiskey and missing puppies blew away.

But then her boots hit the ground and while she was till catching her balance, James came down the chute on his stomach, arms outstretched. Before she could move, he tackled her knees. She stumbled and fell into the soft sand with James on top of her. They were both laughing and their eyes met. There was a long moment so intense it could have turned awkward, but Whiskey saved the day. He grabbed James' belt from behind and pulled. Although James was a tall man, a stubborn 80-pound dog had no trouble dislodging him. He scrambled to his feet and Whiskey continued pulling back-back-back with James lurching after him. Kinney only stopped laughing long enough to find her phone and film it. But when James' jeans came down, and he was standing in his striped boxers, she literally dropped the phone. "Off, Whiskey! Off!"

"Don't tell him to pull my shorts off!" James yelled. "Who knows what he'll savage next."

"Come, Whiskey," she called, almost breathless. Her sides hurt and tears streamed down her cheeks.

Rocky sat near the slide, watching it all. Impassive. Judging. Such hijinks were far beneath him.

"This wasn't a fair fight," James said, pulling up his jeans. "You made out like Whiskey didn't care at all about you. Meanwhile he's a skilled guard dog—the James Bond of canines."

"How was I to know what he'd do?" Kinney said, getting to her feet. "Everything he does is a surprise."

James flung something else on the ground to decoy Whiskey. "Oh yeah? Well here's another surprise."

He rushed at her but she took off, clomping in her boots toward the creek where it curved and flowed around and away from the parking lot.

Before she reached it, she heard a scream. "Help! Help!"

She raced to the bank of the creek. It was deeper here and running faster. In the middle was a woman in a long purple dress. She was floundering and trying to get her footing on slippery rocks. "My dog," she screamed. "My dog."

Flinging off her jacket, Kinney slid down the bank and stepped into the creek. "Where's the dog?"

The woman pointed to a sandbank a few yards away, where a Chihuahua stood shivering, with water rushing past on either side.

"I've got him," Kinney said, wading toward the dog. The current was faster than she expected and the rocks more treacherous. Cold water flooded her boots and drenched her jeans.

"Kinney, wait," James called as he slid down the bank. "Let me do it."

"I'm in now," she said. "Stay dry. And watch Whiskey."

A few more strides got her to the sandbank, where she grabbed the little dog by its sodden blue sweater. She waded back to the bank and handed him to James, who wrapped the dog in her jacket. Then she went back for the woman.

That turned out to be more challenging. She was cold, panicking and flailing wildly. "I can't, I can't."

"Don't make me carry you," Kinney said. "You can walk and you will walk."

The woman took a few faltering steps with Kinney trying to support her. She was about to topple when a black head appeared in the fading light. Whiskey grabbed the woman's dress and started pulling.

"Ow, ow. A wolf!" she screamed.

"It's my dog. Just let him guide you," Kinney said, not knowing what else to do. She wasn't going to fight the dog in the water and risk making things worse.

Bending, the woman grabbed Whiskey's collar and clambered slowly after him to the bank, where James helped them out. Kinney picked her way carefully over the rocks and joined them.

James' hand felt warm as he pulled her out of the water. He took off his jacket to put it around her shoulders, since the Chihuahua was still swaddled in hers. Kinney shook her head and gestured to the woman in the purple dress, who was shivering and crying.

They trailed toward the parking lot, leaving wet footsteps in the sandy soil. "Ma'am, are you okay?" Kinney asked. "How did that happen?"

The woman clutched James' arm. "My dog slipped off the bank," she said through chattering teeth. "I thought it would be easy to get him, but it was awful."

"Everything's going to be fine," he said. "I'll drive you home." He pointed to the two-seater sports car. "Kinney, it's already going to be tight with Rocky and the Chihuahua. Can you drive yourself or should we wait for a cab?"

"I'm fine." She forced herself to stop shaking long enough to smile. "I'm great, actually." She let Whiskey into the back of the Prius. "I've got an amazing dog."

As she drove home, she kept glancing over her shoulder at Whiskey as if he were too good to be true. He was supposedly all hers now. But what if she ended up falling hard for him and the City pulled another fast one? The mayor was always shifting the goalposts.

"I just don't know how to feel about all this, Whiskey," she said.

This time when she looked back, the dog met her eyes. Then he opened his mouth and let out a loud belch from all the water he'd swallowed in the creek.

Laughing, she shook her head. "I couldn't have said it better myself."

CHAPTER TWELVE

The sun had barely crested the horizon when Kinney stopped the Prius near a small park on the outskirts of town several days later. The Tattle Creek neighborhood somehow hadn't made it onto the City's radar yet, as evidenced by the startling lack of bronze statues. Kinney shook her head over the realization that their absence was the first thing you noticed now. No doubt some of the more obscure breeds would start cropping up in bronze before long, with space at a premium downtown. For now, the residents apparently relished their low profile; their gardens were filled with showy spring flowers in non-regulation colors and there was no dog art to be seen.

The neighborhood's low profile was the exact reason she'd chosen it for her solo dog training sessions. Cori and other Mafia members had been visiting Whiskey regularly while she was at work to make sure he was coping okay. They'd taken him out many times and determined that it was safe to walk him in public, but the fewer distractions the better. Cori had given Kinney a very specific training plan that started with providing plenty of exercise and observing his physical reaction to everything he encountered, including men, women, children, dogs, cats, prey animals, sounds, vehicles, and even toys and sticks. The list was long, and she was to send a report to Cori each and every night. Once they had a good understanding of Whiskey's triggers, they could introduce gradual exposure with positive reinforcement.

Inside the small park, she unhooked the dog and let him run. He took off like a shot, which would normally unnerve her, but Cori had assured her that he wouldn't leave his meal ticket. Whatever his shortcomings, his recall was good. Testing it, she called his name and he quickly reappeared at her side. Then she let him go again, smiling as he circled the perimeter, nose to the ground.

She zipped her jacket to her throat, waiting for the sun to chase away the chill. Implementing Cori's plan meant rising at four thirty to put in an hour or two with Whiskey every day before work. Far from feeling resentful, she was excited to get going—to give this beautiful dog the exercise and structure he deserved and truly required, as a working breed. If she could turn him back into the calm, composed creature he was when she saw him first, it would be a huge victory.

When he'd blown off some steam, she went through his basic commands a few times. The dog responded flawlessly to "sit," "down," "stay" and "drop it." He even held a down-stay at a distance, keeping a close eye on her as she circled him. Jacinda, his previous owner, had clearly put in time with him early on. Summoning the dog, she hooked him up, noticing that while he watched her closely from a distance, at her side he would only offer a passing glance, or even stared to one side. It was proof that she hadn't yet earned his trust. That was to be expected, but she needed to be able to attract his attention at all times to avoid trouble. At first she would have to resort to bribes. Pulling liver treats out of her pocket, she walked him back and forth, commanding him to "watch me" and rewarding him when he met her eyes.

Behind her, someone applauded. Turning, she saw a fit young man in jogging gear who was dripping with sweat.

"What are you doing here, Wyatt?" she asked, instantly suspicious. Was Cliff having her watched? And wasn't Madison Parker's camera enough?

"Uh... running in my neighborhood?" he said. "Is there a law against that?"

"Not yet," she said. "I just don't like an audience."

"I don't see why not. You're doing great with this dog. You should be proud."

"Wyatt... nothing personal, but I don't like to think about work outside of work, and when I see you it's inevitable."

"Got it," he said, grinning. "It's a tough environment, Butterfield. That's why I need to run so much."

"And another thing. If you see me outside of work, call me—"

"Kinney," he said. "Got that, too." He turned and loped off, calling over his shoulder, "For the record, I'm not a bad guy."

"I know," she called after him. "Like I said, nothing personal."

When he was out of sight, she proceeded out into the street. The houses were sparse in Tattle Creek, with plenty of property. She would be unlikely to encounter many people at this early hour, but enough to do some initial research. In the meantime, she was to focus on leash protocol. Whiskey had already proven to have better leash manners than she did. He walked calmly by her side, but she clenched the leash and tightened up at the slightest distraction, from a bird to a squirrel. Now she realized she had to observe herself as much as him. Taking a deep breath, she relaxed, so that she wouldn't transmit her anxiety through the leash. That was critical, apparently. Master the leash walk and you've practically mastered the dog, Cori said. It laid the foundation of the relationship and established her as a trustworthy leader providing clear, reliable direction.

Within two blocks, she calmed right down. Whiskey's performance was impeccable. He didn't flinch at passing cars or bicycles. A man trundled by with a kid in a wagon and the dog wagged his tail in greeting. When a cat raced across their path, his ears pricked and his pace picked up, but when she told him to "leave it," he settled right down.

She shook her head. This dog seemed perfect. He was far better behaved than her beloved Kali, despite all the classes and training she poured into her. Golden retrievers were among the smarter breeds, but Kali had nothing on Whiskey. You could see the intelligence in his eyes, even though those eyes rarely settled on her.

An odd feeling pressed on her chest. She wanted this dog to find her worthy of respect. It was strange, because she didn't care nearly as much about what Cliff, Mayor Bradshaw or even Cori thought about her. But she did care about Whiskey's opinion. It wasn't logical, but it was true all the same. She'd seen him at his best and he was a dog whose good opinion meant something.

She found herself wondering if the episode at Myrtle McCabe's had been blown out of proportion. There was no question he'd been nervous at the Barber home, but once he was out of it, perhaps he'd reverted to his old self. She had never been convinced that the nip on her arm had been intentional. He had probably been going for the shovel or the hoe. Nonetheless, with a big dog like this, biting a hoe wasn't permitted either.

Coming around the corner, she barely had time to

register the change in Whiskey's posture. His ears pricked, his entire body stiffened and his eyes locked on a target. She looked to the right just in time to see a tiny white dog careening down a steep driveway. Whiskey darted in front of her to meet the fluffy snowball. "No, leave it," she said, heart pounding. He could swallow this fluffy crumb in one gulp.

Whiskey left it. He stood stock still while the white puppy frisked around his paws, and started leaping into his face. His posture became relaxed, but Kinney's didn't. She was still clutching the leash tightly and had reduced his slack. With a deep breath, she loosened her grip.

Whiskey felt the slack and raced around her to pounce on the puppy. Twice they looped, while she called, "No, no." Finally, she lost her balance and tipped over. Her head connected with something hard and she lay on her side for a second, stunned.

"Oh, my goodness," someone called.

Footsteps slapped toward her and furry pink slippers appeared by her head. A woman in a pink plaid housecoat stood over her and asked, "Are you all right?"

"Get the puppy," Kinney said. "Before he eats it."

The woman laughed. "Take a look. It's more like the other way around."

Kinney rose on one elbow to see Whiskey lying on his back on the sidewalk while the puppy attacked his throat with high pitched growling noises.

"My dear, I'm so sorry. The puppy slipped out while I got the mail."

"It's okay. Everything's okay. I'm just worried about my dog. He isn't always sweet."

"Looks pretty good to me," the woman said. She had a chic brown bob, hazel eyes and a nice smile. "Which is more than I can say for you. You hit your head, I'm afraid, and it's bleeding quite a bit."

"I'm fine, really. I'll just untangle myself and be on my way."

The woman leaned over and took Kinney's arm. "You'll do no such thing. My puppy caused you an injury on my property. I'll clean up that gash and make you a coffee. It's the least I can do."

"Really, it's not necessary." Kinney got to her feet clumsily, trying to unfurl the leash. "I have to get to work soon."

"Well you can't go to work looking like that. And I'm sure you need to be caffeinated." The woman held Kinney's elbow to steady her. "Besides, I really don't think you should be driving quite yet."

Her grip was like a tractor beam. Kinney found herself going up the driveway without realizing her feet were moving. Whiskey followed, and the pup followed Whiskey.

"Is that a bichon?" Kinney asked. "It's very cute."

The woman nodded. "I have a litter of six inside and they're all crazy like this. I can't wait to send them to their new homes. I love to see them come and even more to see them go."

Kinney walked up the stone stairs, feeling a gentle push behind her. The woman was a natural herder. "So you're a breeder?"

"I am. Prepare yourself for the onslaught. There are ten adults as well as the incorrigible litter."

Kinney stopped abruptly at the heavy oak front door. "I can't take Whiskey in there. I don't trust him with other dogs. Or people." She touched the trickle of blood on her forehead and stared at her fingers. "I just adopted him."

The woman turned to look at Whiskey, who was nuzzling the pup with his long nose. "Trust your eyes. I've owned hundreds of dogs in my life and used to breed shepherds. This dog is completely relaxed. And you can trust me to know whether to risk my valuable puppies with him. As long as he's had his shots, we're fine."

"If you say so. I guess."

"I say so. And I'll add that your worrying will create problems, not solve them. Dogs pick up on our thoughts and intentions before we even know we have them."

Inside, they were instantly swarmed by white fluffy dogs, none standing higher than Whiskey's belly.

"What did I tell you?" the woman said, smiling. "All good." She held out her hand. "I'm Marilyn Rossi."

"I've heard of you. Apparently your bichons are the best in Dorset Hills."

"They are." She was more matter-of-fact than arrogant. "I worked very hard to make that true. Now, follow me."

"We can't leave the dogs alone," Kinney protested.

"My house, my rules." Marilyn's tone inspired leadership. Whiskey would probably meet her eyes without a second thought. Maybe it took decades of work with dogs to win that honor.

She led Kinney first to the bathroom, where she told her to sit on the side of the tub. Within just a few minutes, she'd cleaned up the gash with antiseptic and covered it with a bandage. "You'll live," she said. "Now for the coffee and a few minutes to settle your nerves."

Kinney gazed around from a stool at the granite island in the kitchen as Marilyn put on a pot of coffee. "You have a beautiful home."

"I love this place more than I can say. Out here, we're still beneath the mayor's notice and we can ignore the worst of this Dog Town foolishness. At least most of the time. It would break my heart to leave it but—"

"Mom! Where's my backpack? I gotta leave in— Oh." A pretty teen with glossy brown hair in a high ponytail stood in the kitchen doorway. "Who are you?"

"Kinney Butterfield. My dog collided with one of your pups at the end of the driveway and I paid the price."

The girl's brow furrowed and she turned to her mom. "You can't let the dogs outside, Mom. Ever."

Marilyn took a deep breath. "Robin, dogs need to go outside. Obviously. That said, a puppy shouldn't be racing into traffic. She slipped out when I got the mail."

"You need to be more careful." Robin's voice rose and she sounded on the verge of tears.

"I know, I know. Just relax and get yourself some cereal before school, okay?"

The girl flounced off, ponytail swaying, and returned with a man who was still in striped pajamas. "Excuse me," he said. "Robin didn't say we had guests. I'm Keith Rossi."

Kinney introduced herself again. "I tripped outside your house and Marilyn kindly patched me up."

Keith tried to smile and failed. "Marilyn, did one of the pups run out?"

The confident breeder quailed a bit under her husband's gaze. "Everything's fine, Keith. The puppy's safe, and Kinney's brains didn't splatter."

Kinney caught a movement out of the corner of her eye. Whiskey had come to sit beside her stool, and the bichons streamed in after him like a parade of little white brides. Everyone else was too worked up to notice.

"Honey, we need to be extra careful with the dogs right now," Keith said. "Who knows what could happen?"

Robin threw down the backpack she'd found. "I can't live like this. High school is hard enough without being terrified all the time, Mom. I want to move somewhere safe."

Marilyn pressed her lips together as she poured the coffee. "Can we have this discussion later, please? There's no need to bring our guest into this."

"No, it can't wait till later." Robin was working herself into a righteous rage. "Maybe you'll actually listen to me when there's a guest around. I keep trying to tell you that we're not safe here."

Pushing a mug of coffee toward Kinney, Marilyn said, "I'm so sorry. We had a break-in about six weeks ago and everyone's still on edge."

"That's awful." Kinney held the mug tightly with both hands, appreciating its warmth. "What was taken?"

Marilyn locked eyes with Robin to silence her. "Nothing was taken that wasn't returned. We're all fine and there's been nothing amiss since then."

A tremor went through Kinney's hands as she made the connection, and she set the mug down with a clink. "Let me guess: someone stole a puppy. And then gave it back."

There was a collective gasp and a second's silence that confirmed her suspicion.

"How did you know?" Robin came closer to pin Kinney with a stare. "Is it happening all over town? Tell me it's not."

"It's not happening all over." Kinney's voice automatically took on the soothing tone she'd mastered in social work. "I just put two and two together from the conversation." She tapped her forehead beside the bandage. "I'm good like that."

"If you guessed, it must have happened before," Robin persisted. "Our puppy can't be the only one."

"Robin, I work for the Canine Corrections Department. If this were a widespread issue, I would know about it."

The teen put both hands on the counter and leaned in. "Are you saying it never happens?"

She was persistent, but Kinney was skilled at dodging.

"Puppies and dogs go missing here and there in Dorset Hills, but it's not a frequent occurrence. I'm sure you're completely safe here. I noticed you have a security system."

"It's new," Marilyn said. "We hoped everything would settle down after getting it, but as you can see, nerves are still frayed."

"I think we'd be better off moving," Keith said, pouring himself a coffee, since Marilyn didn't offer one. "Dorset Hills was already getting cheesy. Now there's this nasty twist. If a top breeder is getting targeted, what's next?"

Marilyn pressed her lips together as she stirred cream into her coffee. The spoon made a loud clanking noise as everyone fell silent.

Putting her elbows on the counter, Kinney rested her chin on her hands and looked at Robin. "What would make you feel safer here?"

"Nothing," Robin snapped. She turned and rummaged through the cupboard, and then pulled out a granola bar. Her eyes fell on Whiskey, who was now lying in the doorway to the dining room, literally covered in fluffy white pups. One was asleep between his paws. "Your dog looks like the wolf in Bellington Square."

Kinney laughed. "I've thought the same. But he's a sweetheart. Mostly." Taking another sip of coffee, she asked, "Would a wolf like Whiskey make you feel safer?"

Her ponytail tail dipped to one side as she considered. "Maybe."

"Personally, I feel better having a big dog around," Kinney said.

Robin tore open the granola bar, started to take a bite and then changed her mind. "No one would break in if we had a huge German shepherd. Right?"

"Probably not," Kinney said. "Whiskey's bark is terrifying. I think twice about coming into my own house."

Finally, Robin smiled. She took a bite of the granola bar, and chewed. "But he's a good dog, right?" she mumbled through a mouthful.

Kinney nodded. "He's a magnificent dog. Truly. But he's also had some hard times and I need to work on increasing his confidence again."

The teen went over and sat down beside Whiskey. He put his long nose on her leg without a moment's hesitation. The puppies were climbing all over him, but he didn't move an inch.

Kinney looked at Marilyn. "You used to breed shepherds, right?"

Marilyn nodded. "Twenty years ago. They got too much for me. So many big, shedding dogs."

"One big, shedding dog might not be so bad." Kinney smiled over her cup. "I can connect you to a wonderful rescue. You could have a well-trained dog in no time."

Looking from Keith to Robin, Marilyn asked, "Would that help, honey? If we got a big dog like Whiskey?"

Robin gave the last of her granola bar to Whiskey, and then leaned down to kiss him between his big ears. His tail beat happily and he licked her face. "Yeah. If I get to choose the dog, and it's just like Whiskey, I'll stop asking to move."

Marilyn reached across the counter, squeezed Kinney's hand and mouthed, "Thank you."

Getting off the stool, Kinney said, "I've gotta run, but I'm hoping you'll consider participating in the City's breeder showcase at the Fourth of July festival."

Leaving her card on the counter, she collected Whiskey's leash from Robin. Marilyn walked her down to the sidewalk, giving Kinney a chance to say more. Turning, she scanned the street for any sign of Wyatt Cobb, but the coast was clear.

"Do you mind if I ask you for more details about the break-in?" she asked.

"There isn't much more to say, really. Unfortunately, Robin got home first and found the family room window broken. We realized a puppy was missing, and reported it to the CCD. The very next morning, our pup was sitting outside in a cardboard box on a heating pad. Honestly, I assumed a kid did it and his mother forced him to bring it back."

"That sounds plausible," Kinney said. "Did anyone from the City call you about it?"

Marilyn shook her head. "I called them to confirm the pup was home and that was that. But then a few days later, I got a letter approving my request to build an outdoor kennel. I'd been applying for years with no luck so I didn't want to rock the boat by asking more questions. That's a big reason I don't want to move. I'd never get the same chance again."

"Probably not," Kinney said. "I'm so glad you get to stay and expand."

"Thanks to you. I have to put my daughter's needs first, but it would have broken my heart to leave Dorset Hills. Despite how silly it's becoming, it's my home and always has been." She squeezed Kinney's arm again. "Don't take this the wrong way, but I'm so glad you tripped outside my house today."

"Me too," Kinney said, setting off with Whiskey. "I couldn't have banged my head in a better place."

"I hope your day looks up," Marilyn called after her.

"It's already pretty much perfect," Kinney called back, smiling as Whiskey trotted along at her side.

CHAPTER THIRTEEN

Clarence Dayton tried to slam the door closed but Evie was quicker, shoving her foot in the crack. The pink sandal was in remarkably good shape, considering what it went through on Runaway Farm and now during undercover dog police work. Kinney had laughed when Evie called them her "lucky" shoes, but she was starting to reconsider her regulation work boots. Now that she was assigned to reception, her uniform wasn't required and she could probably make an effort to dress a little better. She hadn't worried much about her appearance, either in social work or as a dog cop. Sensible was the name of the game. But now she wondered if she'd been hiding behind her uniform and casual attire. Evie, Remi, Sasha, Ari and Andrea MacDuff managed to be fully engaged with the Rescue Mafia and look great at the same time. It seemed to open doors.

It certainly did today. Evie gave a little squeal and Clarence flung back the old oak door with a resigned sigh. "I thought we finished our business, young lady. I came out of retirement to attend your ridiculous Easter event and apparently helped save a number of exotic animals in the process. Doesn't that earn me some peace?"

"Oh, Clarence," Evie said, as she brushed by him and beckoned to Kinney and Remi. "How can you say no to three lovely ladies who want to visit?"

"Easy," he grumbled. "No. And another thing? No."

"You haven't lost your charm," she said, leading everyone to the kitchen. "Just be glad I brought Kinney Butterfield and Remi Malone instead of Cori."

"I like Cori well enough," he said, following them through his own home. "She mostly leaves me alone and when she shows up she doesn't talk much." He looked around at them. "You're all talkers. I can tell."

"I'm not," Kinney said. "If I go a whole day without saying a word, it's a good day."

"Me too," Remi said. "I have social anxiety."

"And yet you're both talking," he said, shaking his head as he filled the tea kettle. "You must want something. People always want something in Dorset Hills. As if giving up my family's estate and our legacy weren't enough."

"You're right, we do want something," Evie said. "And I'm hoping you want the same thing: to oust Mayor Bradshaw."

The kettle overflowed but he didn't turn off the tap. "Don't play with an old man's heart, Evelyn."

"It's just a hope and dream at this point, Clarence," she said. "I'm hoping you can help us make it a reality."

The three women sat around his oak table in chairs that had been abused by generations of pets. He turned off the faucet, poured out the overflow, and then put the kettle on the stove. After turning the gas on high, he turned. "Now you can talk all you want, ladies."

Kinney put her elbows on the kitchen table. "I work for the CCD, sir."

He raised his hand. "I know that. Let's start by assuming I know just about everything. Being a much-pitied hermit has the effect of bringing out chatty people with casseroles and gossip."

"So, the recluse role is all a ploy," Evie said, smiling. "To keep yourself fed and amused."

"We should have brought a casserole," Remi said, lifting Leo into her lap.

Clarence withered each of them in turn with dark eyes through round spectacles. "Maybe the casserole ladies are hoping for a slice of my inheritance, who knows? You're more likely to get my attention with well-planned plots and schemes."

"It's not much of a plan, as yet," Kinney said. "All we have is a string of stolen puppies. Purebred pups from some of the best breeders in town."

"I didn't see that in the news," he said, turning back to the stove as the kettle squealed.

"The mayor told me right after the Easter festival," Evie said. "But when I asked him about it later, after I got over my concussion, he acted like I was crazy."

Clarence poured hot water into a teapot. "You are crazy... for going to Bill directly. Now he knows you'll start poking around. Because you lovely little hellions can't stop doing that." He dropped teabags into the pot and smirked over his shoulder. "That's the only reason I tolerate you."

Kinney picked up the story. "So, like you said, we started poking around. Four different breeders have lost a puppy and had it returned the next day under mysterious circumstances. One practically admitted the City bought her silence. Two others got sudden approval from the City to expand their kennels, which had been withheld before. There's construction going on at three sites."

"Puppy thefts, buy-offs, and cover-ups, alas." Clarence placed tea cups and saucers on a tray. "It's a bit extreme even for Bill Bradshaw, isn't it?"

Evie nodded. "Very. Keeping breeders quiet won't be easy, even with substantial bribes. Their love of their dogs might even run deeper than love of their kids."

"It should," Clarence said. "Children are just a necessary evil. Dogs are a joy."

"No argument here," Kinney said, smiling. "But so far we haven't found any breeders whose pups didn't come back. And we have no idea at all about possible motives."

"My best guess is that someone wanted to steal the Dog Town magic and use our best bloodlines to bring cachet to a different town," Evie said. "Then when City Hall found out, they probably apprehended the thief and bought off the breeders to keep panic from rising."

Clarence waved away Kinney's gesture of help and carried the tray of rattling china to the table. After he set it down, he shook his head. "Good theory, but you're probably barking up the wrong tree."

"Mr. Dayton, what do you know?" Kinney asked, watching him pour tea with a hand that shook slightly. "We'd love a nudge in the right direction."

Offering the first cup to her, he stared over his glasses. "You're the cop, what does your intuition tell you?"

"That it's something bigger," Kinney said. "It was too neat and clean. The City is always sloppy. The Mafia manages to defeat them almost every time or at least figure out the game. This time it seems like a slick operation."

"The mayor bragged to me about his new advisors," Evie said. "After I turned down the job as chief of staff, he hired someone with no political experience. I couldn't find any dirt on him, though."

"No dirt just means he knows how to cover his tracks," Kinney said. "There's no such thing as clean politics."

Remi shifted Leo in her lap, continuously stroking his ears. "Clarence, did you hear about missing puppies?"

He sipped his tea and smiled. "Just a whisper or six. And then they faded away, just as you said."

"So there are more than we know about," Kinney said. "Maybe some pups haven't been returned."

Clarence pinched a sugar cube with little tongs and dropped it into his tea. "Possibly."

Evie gripped her delicate cup in both hands and her white knuckles made Kinney fear she'd break the china. "If we could expose this cover-up, we might be able to garner public support to oust the mayor."

"Don't get my hopes up," Clarence said. "I'm on borrowed time already."

A meow at Kinney's feet startled her. A calico cat wove through her boots in a sinuous figure eight. Smiling, she scooped up the purring cat. She'd always had a soft spot for felines and had planned on getting one until Whiskey came along.

"That's Ramona," Evie said, releasing her chokehold on the teacup to pat the cat.

Ramona gave Kinney a headbutt, and then another and a third. "It's like she's trying to tell me something," she said.

"Three headbutts ought to do it," Clarence said. "For the sake of earning back my solitude, I'll help her out: you're thinking too small, all of you. The mayor's schemes were more contained before. You need to look at the forest, not the trees."

After Ramona settled in her lap, Kinney leaned across

the table toward Clarence. "You know more, Mr. Dayton, I know you do."

He stared into his tea for a moment. "I value my privacy more than anything, as you know. Getting involved goes against the grain."

"What'll it take?" Kinney asked. "For you to help us see the forest?"

His eyes rose to meet hers. "If you help me, Miss Butterfield, I'll help you."

"Of course. What can I do?"

"Marilyn Rossi brought me a nice tuna casserole the other day," he said. "She told me you used some mediation kung fu on her daughter and the girl's been a delight ever since." He took another sip before adding, "Was that a one-off, or are you really that skilled at negotiation?"

Kinney leaned back in her chair, running her hands over Ramona's warm body. It was too bad dogs didn't come with a purr as well; it was very comforting. "I always thought mediation could be my superpower if I had more opportunity," she said.

"I'll give you that opportunity. I want the City to give me back decision-making control of the Dayton Estate. I want the last word on how it's developed and used. They're waiting for me to die so they can build a condo on the land, which is why it's been left to practically go to seed. My grandfather was an honorable man and his legacy deserves to be honored, too."

"I'd love to, sir, but I'm afraid my name is mud right now. I've been demoted for adopting a reactive dog, and I'm being publicly shamed in a remedial training class. The mayor's office isn't going to listen to me."

He waved his hand. "I'm sure you'll find a way. You're resourceful and you have integrity."

Evie poured herself more tea. "I think I can get you in the door, Kinney."

Kinney pushed her chair back so that she had room to bend and give Ramona a kiss between her ears. She loved the scent of cat, especially since she'd owned shedding dogs that tended to smell like, well, dog.

"Count me in," she said. "If we can get a meeting, I will work whatever mediation magic I have."

Clarence's smile came out in full for the first time, and it was unexpectedly charming. "Wonderful. Now come back to me in a few days and I'll see what secrets the casseroles have revealed about the missing puppy plot." He got up and led them to the door. "Just you, Miss Butterfield. Too much girl power jangles my nerves."

"LET'S pop in and see Sasha," Evie said, as they left the Puccini Café after lunch. It had been nice to hang out like regular people for a change. It always seemed like they were on one mission or another, catching up on their lives in stolen moments.

"I need to get home to Whiskey," Kinney said. "I booked the day off so we could do some extra training. I've got Miracle Makeover class tonight and an assignment with James."

"All the better," Evie said, weaving through crowded noon sidewalks. "This is so well-timed."

Main Street was always busy but the sunshine brought out the throngs—some with dogs, and others wanting to see those dogs. There were new brass structures shaped like circus poodles outside the shops that had hooks to hold leashes. You could leave your dog outside without worry in Dorset Hills. At least, that used to be true.

"What's well-timed?" Kinney asked, still staring at the brass poodles. "I've got too many mysteries on my mind already, Evie."

"Barbet!" Remi shouted, pointing. "French water dog. Non-shedding. Field retriever and excellent companion dog. Rare phantom coloring."

Evie patted her arm. "No need to be nervous, Remi."

"Who said I'm nervous?"

"You always start shouting rare dog breeds when you're flustered," Evie said "It's endearing. Just give Leo a squeeze and all will be fine."

"Okay, now *I'm* getting nervous," Kinney said, as Evie pulled open the door to The Model Dog grooming salon. "What are you plotting now, Evie?"

"Just relax," Sasha said, smiling a greeting from behind the counter. She had blonde curls, a pretty face, and a compact build. Her blue lab coat covered what appeared to be a grey knit dress, over matching suede boots. "This is an oasis of calm for dogs and humans."

Lifting her nose, Kinney sniffed. "Lavender?"

"The most soothing scent." Sasha came around the counter to help Kinney out of her coat. "Thanks for dropping by. There's something I want you to see in the back."

"Why am I the only one losing her coat?" Kinney asked. "I smell a set-up under all the lavender."

Sasha pulled Kinney into the back room. "Make her a tea, Remi, will you?"

"I've had enough tea," Kinney said. "I prefer coffee anyway."

"Hard on the nerves," Sasha said. "Enough coffee and you give off shocks."

"Good, then maybe you'll let go of my arm."

They walked past two grooming areas and into a small room at the back. Inside, an old, cracked leather swivel chair sat like a throne.

Sasha gestured for Kinney to take a seat. "You remember my former life, right? I used to be a hairstylist for humans, rather than dogs. Now I only cut for friends, and you're the only one who hasn't been introduced to my scissors."

Kinney clutched the big knot of hair at the back of her head. "I'm fine. I only get it cut once a year."

Clucking sadly, Sasha slipped a robe over Kinney's T-shirt and jeans. "That's not good for woman nor beast. And a little bird told me you might have a high-profile meeting at the mayor's office. I know from experience that he's swayed by personal presentation."

"The meeting isn't even set up." Kinney's voice was shrill. "I highly doubt he'll say yes."

Evie held up her phone. "His office says it's a go. He must be highly invested in whisking Clarence out of the way."

Kinney sank into the salon chair, mostly because her knees got weak. "Oh no. I didn't think he'd agree."

"That's how we all grow," Evie said, leaning against the wall. "Overstretch, overcommit and then make it work."

Remi put Leo in Kinney's lap. "It's just hair, Kinney. Your whole identity doesn't ride on it."

Maybe not, but she preferred to blend in. That way she could observe, rather than be observed. Looking too good would blow her cover. On the other hand, the mayor most certainly did judge based on appearances, and she was determined to hold up her end of the bargain for Clarence. If looking pretty swayed the vote, she'd suck it up.

Sensing the shift, Sasha picked up her scissors. "Just close your eyes and pat Leo. It'll all be over in a few minutes. You have beautiful hair and all it needs is some shape."

Kinney did as she was told and patted Leo, focussing on his ears. The satiny flaps got stroked so much they'd fall off one day if Remi didn't get stingy with his attention.

When Sasha gave her the all-clear, she opened her eyes and gasped. The so-called shaping had lopped a good eight inches. She'd barely be able to scrabble a bun together. "It's too short," she said.

Evie shook her head. "It's gorgeous. Once you get a good blowout, it'll be spectacular." She opened a drawer in a little cabinet and pulled out a palette of makeup. "Let me give you a few pointers, for bringing out your eyes."

Kinney tried to bat her away but Leo was clinging on for dear life on the slippery salon robe. "My eyes are fine."

"Better than fine, but people don't do enough with dark eyes," Evie said. "You can totally go dramatic."

There were quick footsteps outside and the curtain drew back. It was Andrea MacDuff, more commonly known as Duff. Of all the Mafia associates, she was the most sophisticated. Her auburn hair fell in a sleek bob and her navy suit was both polished and functional. As always, she had stylish pumps, and no doubt a matching bag, although it was concealed in an armful of clothing.

"I was cleaning out my closet and brought over a few things," she said. "We're about the same size, Kinney, and I know you prefer not to be showy. I've got a few things that might fit the bill."

Kinney let out a huge sigh that nearly blasted the eyebrow comb from Evie's hand. "Oh my gosh, are we in high school again? I feel like the ugly duckling getting a makeover to win the handsome prince."

Evie yanked out a few errant hairs, causing Kinney to

yelp. "Oh honey, you've already won James, the handsome prince. But you've still got to worry about the prince of darkness. Or more specifically, the Mayor of Mayhem."

Remi handed Kinney a cup of coffee. "Remember, even Cori dresses for the cause when needed."

Somehow, that helped quell Kinney's nerves. "True. If Cori can be a hypocrite for puppies, I certainly can."

"That's the spirit," Evie said, applying eyeliner with a steady, heavy hand. "This is just a trial run for the meeting. We'll review everything again when it's set, and go over strategies, too."

"It's such a great opportunity," Remi said. "Maybe you can bat those eyelashes and find out what's happening with the missing puppies."

"Eyelashes are a powerful weapon," Evie said. "Don't ever forget that this town is more about style than substance. But substance wins in the end."

Kinney groaned as the wand poked the corner of her eye, and Leo licked her chin to tell her it would all be okay.

CHAPTER FOURTEEN

"Where are you taking us?" Kinney asked, bracing herself with one hand on the dashboard of James' SUV. It turned out, perhaps unsurprisingly for a billionaire, that he had vehicular options. The little sports car from their previous Magical Makeover class had been replaced with something that allowed the dogs to be separated. Rocky lay in lionlike repose in the back seat, while Whiskey watched the town whiz past from the gated cargo area. He'd suggested they carpool after Cori released them for their latest class assignment, and she couldn't think of a good reason to say no, other than that she always preferred being behind the wheel.

"It's a surprise," James said, with an enigmatic smile that looked foreign on his normally open face. He wasn't a man of mystery, and she liked that about him. There was enough uncertainty at work and in the world at large. She'd had her fill of complicated men and planned to stay single for the foreseeable future. A nice, simple friendship with a good guy was exactly what she needed.

"I don't like surprises. There's a lot to be said for predictability."

He gave her the side-eye. "You're joking, right? You jumped into a creek to save a Chihuahua the other night. You just adopted a traumatized dog after he bit you. Hardly predictable."

She looked out the window to hide her grin. "I guess."

"And then there's the dangerous antics you and the Rescue Mafia take on. If the war stories I hear are true—"

"Highly exaggerated. The Mafia is shrouded by urban myth. We're just a group of nice women. Kind of like a book club, but no reading required."

He laughed. "You might as well admit you're a thrill seeker like the rest of them. After your exploits at Hannah's farm, I think you're all superheroes, or celestial beings."

Kinney's laugh came out like a sputter. "That's gotta be the first time Cori Hogan's been called an angel."

"Maybe not her. Is a vengeful sprite celestial?"

"I'll ask next time book club convenes."

He gave her another sideways glance. "You look awfully nice, tonight. Did Cori implement a dress code without telling me?"

Sighing, Kinney smoothed her already smooth hair. "The girls spruced me up for meeting with the mayor. But he's already postponed it."

"A meeting with the mayor? About what?"

She managed to dodge the question when something caught her eye in the side mirror. "James, take evasive maneuvers. Madison's on our tail."

"With pleasure," he said, turning right at the Dalmatian and slipping quickly into an alley behind the fire station. They stayed there until her funky little red car passed and then he backtracked for a bit.

"She should pick a tamer ride if she wants to sneak around," Kinney said. "But it works in our favor."

After a few moments of silence, James continued, as if they hadn't been diverted. "Just try to take it easy on my sister for now, okay? I worry about the baby. On the other hand, she's totally transformed since she moved home, and it's not just farm life. It's like she's burning with a fiery purpose."

Kinney nodded. "She does look celestial, or at least what I figure that looks like. I attributed it to pregnancy."

"I guess it's a perfect storm of baby, farm animals, Mafia craziness, and true love. Nick practically follows her around with outstretched arms, ready to catch her if she falls."

Kinney's face lit up now and she smiled. "That's pretty darned sweet."

"The love of a good woman does that to a man." His blue eyes flashed in her direction. "That's our fiery purpose."

Tingles rolled up her spine. At the same time, her stomach clenched in fight-or-flight mode. She held her breath till both subsided. The last time someone gave her tingles, she'd ended up heartbroken... and broke. Her ex-boyfriend had secretly spent their scanty savings on shady investments before he packed up and left. He'd tried to take Kali, too, but she'd prevailed in the end, only to face the dog's eventual illness and expenses alone. He wasn't the only deadbeat in her past, either. So, no... she wasn't open to tingles anymore.

"Look at that," she said, swivelling in her seat. "There's a Kerry blue terrier."

The bronze statue was already behind them when James said, "How can you tell? Half of them look the same to me."

"It's all in the groom. Most purebreds have an approved cut, even the Tibetan mastiff. The mayor's personal bronze artist deserves a lot of credit for getting it right most of the time."

Pulling into a parking lot, James said, "We can walk from here."

She looked around and the light dawned. "Craven Road. What a great idea! It's closed to street traffic and we can walk the dogs up and down easily."

Cori had assigned them to use what they'd learned about motivation to get their dogs to meet their eyes on request and focus. Attention was the absolute building block of the bond, she said, and until it came naturally, they had to establish the habit and reinforce through repetition. She'd told them to find someplace to practice with moderate distractions. Everything depended on a slow build.

"I've loved this street ever since Remi gave us the tour last Labor Day," he said, letting Rocky out and putting him into a sit, while she released Whiskey from the back. "It's everything I wanted Dorset Hills to be—quaint, quirky and warm."

Kinney loved it, too. The Craven Road Committee really pushed their luck with the City. They flouted many official neighborhood regulations and all of the unofficial ones. Where most of Riverdale had uniformity in terms of gardens, decorations and even architectural design, Craven Road was a riot of color year-round. One side of the street had a tall fence separating it from the railway tracks. Residents constantly created new art on the fence—painting, mosaics and even textile. Often, there was a subversive tone to the art itself. Today there was a painting, two panels wide, with Noah's ark sinking under the weight of huge bronze dogs. That one wouldn't last, Kinney knew. A lot of good work vanished by night when saboteurs visited with pails of white paint.

The street was still fairly quiet, as families in the mishmash of renovated cottages finished dinner and homework.

Before long, kids and dogs would pour back outside to enjoy the long evenings. Parents on Craven seemed to limit electronic devices and encourage kids to join games like street hockey, basketball or even skipping contests. Some parents sat on porches keeping an eye on everyone, but mostly the kids were left to be kids.

"It's like taking a trip in a time travel machine," James said, urging Rocky along. The dog's default gear was first, although he'd proven himself capable of speed during hide and seek the other night. Generally, he conserved his energy and his enthusiasm. "This is what it was like when Hannah and I were growing up. That's why we both had a homing device that called us back when New York got too much."

"I know what you mean, even though I didn't grow up here." Kinney watched Whiskey trot along briskly, his eyes everywhere except on her. After their teamwork in Clover Park, she'd hoped they'd rounded a corner. Instead he was back to ignoring her as much as possible. "When I moved to Dorset Hills, it was still in its formative stage. I loved its eccentric charm and I found my tribe quickly. Then everything got weird, and we've been trying to recover those peaceful days ever since."

James told Rocky to "watch me," and when that failed, tried to get the dog's attention with various sounds, gestures and facial contortions. "Ever feel like you don't exist?"

Kinney laughed. "I flicker in and out of Whiskey's awareness. It's very humbling."

"It sure is. I can hold every eye in a conference room but I can't get my own dog to look at me." His expression was baffled and more than a bit embarrassed. "How did I not see that my dog doesn't give a crap about me? And why does it sting so much?"

She nodded in sympathy. "It does sting. I'm still on my

honeymoon with Whiskey, but I had the same problem with my previous dog, Kali. She only acknowledged me at around age three." She snapped her fingers at Whiskey and sighed. "The common denominator, unfortunately, is me."

"But you're so good with other dogs," James said. "Not to mention farm animals. I noticed that Alvina the alpaca can't get enough of you. It's like you rolled in clover, or whatever it is she eats."

"I take a lot of pride in being one of the few Alvina hasn't spit on," Kinney said. "But I can't pass the Fourth of July test with an alpaca on a lead."

"I worry about that test," James said. "If they ban Rocky from Dog Town, I don't know what I'll do. I can't leave Hannah to handle a baby and the shenanigans at the farm. But I won't surrender Rocky, either."

"It's still early days," Kinney said, pulling Whiskey's tennis ball out of her pocket. "I truly put my faith in Cori, and if she says we can turn it around, we will."

At the rustle of the tennis ball, Whiskey looked up fast. His beautiful, intelligent eyes lit up, but they were fixed on the ball, not her. Holding the ball up to eye-level, she said, "Watch me." Then she let him take the ball and carry it for a few moments before reclaiming it and repeating the exercise.

"Good job," James said, pulling a small plastic bag out of his pocket. Plucking a small square from the bag, he said, "Watch me," to Rocky. When the dog obeyed, he gave him the treat. "Good boy." He used the high-pitched enthused tone Cori recommended for praise, but it sounded odd coming from James.

"Oh, wow," Kinney said, moving away. "That reeks."

"Do you know what tripe is? Cow guts. I had to look it up. I guess that's why it's so foul." He looked up at her, his eyes pained. "I have to shower after every training session.

Even then I think it still impregnates my clothes. And my hair. Sometimes I wake in the night and smell it."

She tried to repress a grin and failed. "Have you tried latex gloves?"

He nodded. "Rocky wouldn't consider accepting it from latex fingers. Honestly. This dog destroyed my masculine allure in just a week."

"I highly doubt that," Kinney said. "Evie said you get the most fan mail of anyone on The Princess and the Pig. Other than Alvina, of course."

"Well, they can't smell me, can they? It would be a different story in person. Even you—my partner in crime—are walking ahead of me."

She fell back in step. "I can take it. I think you're flattering yourself, actually, because I've smelled far worse."

"Thanks," he said, grinning. "I think."

"You may have more trouble with the society belles," she added, as her eyes watered from the stench. "Probably wouldn't go over so well at the galas."

He shrugged. "I try to avoid those. I find a suit too constrictive these days. Overalls are becoming more my style." He gave her a sideways glance. "I'm done with society belles, too. Give me someone authentic."

The tingle went up her spine again and this time it exploded in a shower of tiny sparks. Why on earth would someone like James choose her? He might *think* he wanted the authentic girl next door, but he was high on nostalgia and farm manure. That would wear off soon enough and he'd need someone classy on his arm. That would never be her. Despite the new haircut and fresh face of makeup, she was still Kinney Butterfield, the girl who barely made it out of a dingy suburb to attend college on scholarship. She was the first person in her family to get a real education, and her mom's eyebrows were still permanently raised in shock. Kinney often had nightmares of getting sucked back there.

She turned to James and gave him her best "friendly" smile. "This stage will pass, and the stench will fade. The girls will be beating down your door."

He focused on Rocky, getting a consistently good response to his command. Finally he turned again. "I think I'm actually winning this battle. And if I can get Rocky to like me, I might win you over too."

She laughed. "If I weren't so focused on Whiskey and work, maybe you could. Don't take it personally."

He gave his billion-dollar smile. "Not at all." He plucked another tidbit out of the bag and dangled it. "Would you like some tripe?"

She dodged away, gagging. "James, stop."

He chased her for a few steps, hauling Rocky along. The dog made it clear that this wasn't worth running for.

Catching her sleeve in a hand sticky with tripe, he stopped her. The street lights flickered on, and at the same moment, the thousands of twinkle lights that Craven Road residents draped over trees, bushes, and everything else burst into glory as well. She stared up at James and saw a halo of lights around his dark hair. Blinking a few times, she found the halo still there. Everything else faded, even the smell of tripe.

A child's scream broke her trance. They turned almost as one and ran toward the sound.

Near the opposite end of the street, where the fence ended and scrub bush began, a small girl with blonde pigtails stood crying. "My dog! He chased a squirrel and now I can't find him."

"Don't worry, we'll help." Kinney held up her hand for

silence as James knelt beside the child. "I hear him. Can you?"

The girl stopped crying and listened. "Yes! That's Buster."

"Okay, we'll get him back. Don't worry." Parents gathered rapidly, and they left the little girl in their custody. Feeling a tug at the end of her leash, Kinney looked down to see Whiskey practically dancing. She gave him some slack. "Find him, Whiskey."

The dog may not have known the command, but he did what came naturally. Pulling Kinney forward, Whiskey plunged into the bushes.

James followed, tugging Rocky. "Why do I feel like I've been conscripted into the Rescue Mafia?"

"Wrong place right time," she said. "That's how it usually begins."

Rocky collapsed on his side and let out huffing sounds of protest. "He's not Mafia material," James said. "Spontaneity isn't his forte."

Whiskey didn't need canine backup. He picked his way gracefully through the bushes, long nose to the ground. Apparently herding wasn't his only talent.

Kinney followed his lead until he stopped in front of a rusted metal culvert. He stuck his head inside and whined. A frantic yapping echoed back.

"We've got ears on Buster," Kinney called back to James, who was trying to push Rocky onto his paws. Dropping to her knees, she shone her phone flashlight into the tube. "And now eyes. There's a Jack Russell terrier about ten yards in. From the way he's squirming, I'd guess he's stuck. Maybe his collar got snagged."

"We'd better call for help." James finally resorted to tripe to get Rocky on his pins. "CCD or Animal Services?"

She studied the culvert and then rose. "It's almost dusk. By the time they get out here, he may have strangled himself." Shrugging off the suit jacket she'd borrowed from Duff earlier, she unhooked Whiskey's leash and after a moment's thought, shoved it down her shirt and into her bra.

"What are you doing?" James asked.

"Going in. I won't let a dog strangle on my watch."

"Kinney, let me." He left Rocky to collapse again. "You went through enough in the creek the other night."

She shook her head. "You wouldn't fit, James. Besides, this is my job. Or at least, it's supposed to be." She got down on hands and knees, and looked inside again. "It's not that far. As long as the dog's not hurt, it'll be a piece of cake."

The false bravado faded about two yards into the culvert. She wasn't a big fan of dark, confined spaces, but then who was? It was like a corrugated tubular coffin. That much, she'd expected. What surprised her was the smell. It was hard to believe that anything could stink more than the tripe James had been brandishing, but there was indeed something worse: death. Something had crawled in here and turned the culvert into an actual coffin. A possum, perhaps. Luckily, there was nothing visible in the stretch between her and Buster.

Breathing through her mouth, she inched forward on her elbows, glad she'd worn a long-sleeve T-shirt. The tube seemed airless, but she knew it opened somewhere else not too far away. It was just her imagination. The trick to getting this done was to stay out of her head.

"Buster, baby," she cooed. "I'm coming for you, boy. Don't you worry. I know it's scary to be stuck in here with a corpse but it's okay. You and I will not add to the pile of bones. We're getting out, I promise you."

The dog whined, but the level of hysteria had leveled

down. Jack Russells were fierce warriors, but they were clever, too.

"Do you know I'm not even getting paid for this?" she muttered, pulling herself along with her elbow and the fingers of whichever hand wasn't holding her phone. She felt one nail break and then another. "I'm on desk duty, now. No one will ever know about my heroic efforts."

She paused to catch her breath, while trying not to smell the decay. It was slimy and damp in here, too. If she allowed herself to think about it, this would rival her worst rescues with the Mafia. But she blocked it out and inched forward again.

"Here's the thing, though, Buster. We'll put a smile on that little girl's face. She'll hug you so hard your ribs might crack. And that is all the reward I need. Tomorrow you'll be the king of Craven Road again."

Finally she got within reach of the dog. She shone the light around to see where he was stuck. Sure enough, he'd snagged the tags of his collar on a spike poking through the corrugated metal. It had just enough of a crook to hold the dog back.

Then she passed the light up and down his body and made sure there were no obvious injuries. Last, she checked his expression and posture. She'd been bitten once recently and she didn't intend to let it happen again. Buster looked friendly enough and his tailed thumped a couple of times on the metal.

"Easy," she said, reaching out tentatively with the leash. Hooking it to his collar, she released the tag from the stake and then tugged gently. "Reverse, soldier."

It wasn't much easier pushing back out, especially with raw elbows and hands, but the decay seemed to propel her on. She could see the shape of something large and lifeless ahead in the tunnel, but deliberately turned the beam away. It seemed indecent.

Finally, she felt large hands on her ankles and someone pulled her back gently. James helped her to her feet and kept his arm around her, even after she surrendered the leash into the little girl's hands. As expected, the girl crushed the wriggling dog in a huge hug. Her parents came over and tried to shake Kinney's hand, and looked horrified instead at her bloody fingers. Looking down, she realized she was filthy and covered in something slick, dark and vile. She tried to move away from James but he wouldn't let go.

It was dark now, and it took a few seconds before she noticed a crowd of at least 20 people and nearly as many cell phones held high. Someone started to clap, and then everyone else followed suit.

"No need for that," Kinney called. "You'd all do the same, right? Buster's your neighbor."

Everyone laughed, voices overlapping as they explained Buster was the clown and trickster of Craven Road; this wasn't his first or worst dangerous exploit. Offers of wine and whiskey drifted out on the chilly air.

"Whiskey!" Kinney said. "Where's my dog?"

A man came forward with Whiskey and Rocky, both dogs walking beautifully and calmly on leashes. "They were good," he said, passing a leash to Kinney.

"I'll take that drink," she said. "Make it a double."

Another voice boomed over the murmuring crowd. "She'll decline that, thanks."

Someone turned a light on the man, but Kinney already knew who it was because her bones had melted in fear in a way they hadn't in the tunnel.

Cliff Whorley stepped forward and grabbed her firmly by one aching elbow.

"Hey! Get your hands off her," James said.

Cliff dropped her arm and backed away, but Kinney slipped out of James' grasp and followed, as if pulled by invisible strings. Once they were beyond the crowd, she said, "Why are you here?"

He started to say "duh" but settled for an eye roll. "It's all over social media. Imagine my surprise when my wife showed me a livestream video of the CCD's receptionist trying to be a hero."

"Cliff, the dog's collar was stuck. Anyone else would have done the same."

"Anyone else would have called *us* to do the job properly." He gestured to a man cloaked in shadows who stepped forward and raised a hand sheepishly. Wyatt Cobb.

"I got the dog out before he strangled himself. You guys would have been half an hour." Her voice had a shrill edge. She hadn't expected him to welcome her back to her old job, but a polite acknowledgment would have been nice. "The owners are happy, the dog's happy. What's the problem?"

His arms crossed over his bulging belly. "The problem is that you showed poor judgement. *Again.* I gave you a second chance—not even counting the stunts you get up to with your friends—and you blew it."

Her throat tightened. It was as bad as being in the tube, only without the putrid decay... unless you counted the slow death of her career. "What are you saying?"

"I'm saying you're suspended, Butterfield." He turned and walked away with Wyatt, calling back, "Spend some time meditating to get your brain straight. The mayor swears by that shiz."

CHAPTER FIFTEEN

The 12-year-old lime-green van took the bumps hard, eliciting squeals and groans in various pitches from its passengers. The mid-June day was perfect for a ride in the country, even if the ride itself was far from perfect.

"Bridget, can you slow down a bit?" Kinney asked, from the back seat. "My head is already aching."

"I've got to keep things rolling," Bridget said. "Otherwise the engine stalls out. If you want a smooth ride you chose the wrong chariot. Ari's swank SUV was an option."

The 10 women had divided up, with Bridget, Cori, Remi and Evie with Kinney in the van, and Nika, Duff, Maisie and Sasha following with Ari. They'd all taken the day off work for this mission. Except for Kinney, who now had all her days off work.

"Do you want a painkiller?" Remi asked, letting Leo inch his way from her lap onto Kinney's. He always knew who needed his help most in any situation. "I have some in my purse."

Kinney shook her head and winced at the sharp pinch behind her eyes. "I might as well weather it through." She looked down at Leo and almost smiled. He'd managed to get most of his body off Remi's lap and onto hers. Remi had volunteered to take the middle seat, with the worst springs. It was the sign of a true friend. "It would ease my pain to kill Cliff Whorley. Figuratively speaking."

Cori turned from the passenger seat and grinned. "An admirable sentiment. When we take down the mayor, Cliff will go with him."

"It could have been worse," Bridget said. "After a dose of Leo, you'll see that."

Resting one hand on Leo's head, she caught Bridget's eye in the review mirror. "I suppose. I could have been fired outright. On camera."

"You were suspended with pay," Bridget said. "That probably only happened because of the cameras."

"Agreed," Evie said, from the other side of Remi. "It's hard to fire someone who's on the front page of the Dog Town newspaper bloodied and triumphant after saving a dog."

Cori braced herself with one gloved hand on the driver's seat and craned around again. "Look at it this way: it's a paid vacation."

Kinney gave a snort. "It's on my employment record. They'll say I was insubordinate, impulsive and—"

"Insufferable," Cori supplied. "I get that one a lot. But I consider all of those high praise." She gave Kinney a rare smile. "It's all about reframing. Do you want to be a yes-man who does the CCD's bidding no matter if it makes sense or not? Or do you want to do the right thing for animals in Dorset Hills and get used to some name-calling?"

"I don't see why I can't do the right thing for animals in Dorset Hills without getting unfairly sanctioned."

Cori turned back, flipping an orange finger on the way.

"Has your short-term memory failed? Since Mr. Bradshaw took office, the price of doing the right thing for Dog Town keeps rising. So how about you quit whining and spend your paid vacation rehabilitating Whiskey and investigating the stolen puppy situation?"

Kinney stroked Leo's head in resignation. If he was the only one offering sympathy, she'd take it. There was no denying that his smooth ears and warm body had a soothing effect. It was probably better than medicine.

"Okay, you're right," she said, after watching the green hills flash past for a few minutes. "I'll end my pity party right here. At least I don't have to organize the Fourth of July festival anymore. Plus I'm lucky to be living nearly rent free at Marti Forrester's house. Maybe by the time this ends, I can figure out what I'm really meant to do. This was never my dream job."

Evie leaned around Remi again. "You're an amazing dog cop, Kinney, but it's time for the next big thing. You know I've had nine lives in the political realm and even though my therapy dog program idea got put on ice, I couldn't be happier." She held up her video camera. "There are so many ways to contribute to this town—even by exposing its seedy underbelly."

"Most of us have been fired before," Cori said. "You adapt. Freelance is better for the attitudinally challenged, like you."

There was a chorus of protests, and Kinney's voice wasn't even the loudest.

"It's a compliment," Cori added. "And a ticket to freedom."

The van hit a big bump and Cori's shiny dark head appeared above the headrest for a moment. She landed with a thud but she didn't make a murmur of complaint. There was no denying that she practiced what she preached. When the road smoothed out again, she said, "Tell us exactly what Clarence said last night. Leave out no detail."

"I'm surprised Clarence would share anything when the mayor's office keeps postponing your meeting," Evie said. "Either he has faith we'll prevail, or he wants to sort out this puppy problem, too."

Running one hand through tangled hair and the other over Leo, Kinney frowned. "I just hope I remember everything. I'd had a drink or three after getting home from Craven Road and he served me another when I cabbed over there."

"Which explains the headache," Bridget offered, eyes crinkling in the rearview mirror.

"Maybe. Either way, you have to be sharp with Clarence and read between the lines. He doesn't like to make things too easy."

"True that," Evie said.

"I always understand him," Cori said. "But I am a little smarter than the average bear."

Kinney withered her with a look from behind.

"I feel that," Cori said.

Even Kinney laughed. Then she closed her eyes for a second to focus on her conversation with Clarence. "Okay, so he did some delicate digging with his casserole confidantes, and apparently there are more stolen puppies than we know about, or were reported. And not all of them have been returned."

Several of the women gasped in shock, but Bridget was the first to speak. "Why wouldn't breeders report their missing puppies?"

Kinney shrugged. "Clarence could only speculate that whoever is stealing them offered good compensation. Maybe they bought off the breeders before they could call it in."

"This is awful," Remi said, reaching for Leo's back paw and holding it. "What are they doing with these puppies? Are they safe?"

"Your guess is as good as mine," Kinney said. "I can't think of a reason anyone would hurt a puppy in Dog Town, especially pedigreed pups. But we need to get to the bottom of this."

Cori had turned to catch every nuance. "Clarence thinks the City is behind it?"

"He does. Otherwise breeders would be screaming to high heaven. Presumably they've been fed some line about how their sacrifice will be for the greater good of Dog Town."

Bridget shook her head. "If so, the City may be hand-picking victims based less on bloodlines than on breeder gullibility."

"Or greed," Cori said. "Plenty of them would forfeit a dog for the right price, as long as they believed that the pup would be safe. And the City could provide that kind of reassurance."

"Clarence didn't press for details for fear of setting off alarms," Kinney said.

Rubbing her forehead, Evie said, "Something feels really strange about this. It's almost as if they're *trying* to confuse us. Throw us off the trail."

"I wish we were that big a threat," Bridget said. "Mostly they just swat us away like flies from the growing decay of Dog Town."

"All we can do is follow the breadcrumbs and see where they take us," Kinney said. "I don't know if this is a real clue from Clarence or conjecture, but he suggested we investigate properties where puppies might be stashed. Hence, our road trip."

Evie leaned forward. "How did you settle on the sites we're visiting?"

Kinney grinned. "Cliff didn't think to lock me out of the CCD system till this morning. So I poked around and found new kennel licences had been issued for three properties outside the city proper but still in Dorset Hills County. Each was listed under a separate name, but I couldn't find anyone with those names. The breeds identified with the new kennels are really unusual: Norwegian lundehund, the Peruvian Inca orchid, and the Thai ridgeback."

"Seriously?" Evie said. "That's not consistent with the new breeder legislation the City was developing. No one breeding Norwegian puffin hunters would be able to waltz in and get a permit to build."

"There was no other public record," Kinney said. "It looked like everything was being done on the down-low, but I didn't get much further before the big red "Access Denied" appeared and my paid vacation began."

"Well done," Bridget said. "That was good sleuthing, Kinney."

"Maybe that's my next career," Kinney said. "Private investigator."

"Public instigator, more like," Cori said. "When you quit bragging, you'll see we're almost at site number one."

Signalling far in advance so Ari could follow, Bridget turned left onto a dirt road. They drove about half a mile over roads that made Kinney nauseated before an old farmhouse came into view. From the front, it was nothing special. In fact, it looked long-vacated. There were no curtains, other than torn lace hanging from an upstairs window.

For the moment, the house appeared to be a front, because all the action was going on to the rear. There was a roar of heavy machinery and a cloud of dust rose like a mushroom. Several cars were parked in a haphazard way in an open field to the right.

"Pull the van into the bushes," Kinney said. "I'm going to sneak around and take a look."

"Like a lime-green van is going to be camouflaged anywhere," Cori said. "Bridget, drop us off, drive back to the main road and we'll text you when we're done."

Kinney preferred to direct her own investigation but when Cori issued orders, she tended to fall in line, too. Things just worked better that way.

Once the van was out of sight, Cori picked her way through the bush in a wide arc. Instead of going closer, she patted a tall, old wall made of rocks and cement. "Boost me."

Kinney gave her a lift up, but Cori didn't stop there. She ran along the wall a few yards and then started climbing a mid-sized oak tree. She was as agile as a monkey, and it wasn't long before she gave Kinney the thumbs-up. Pulling binoculars out of a pouch at her waist, she scanned the area. Then she used her phone to take some photos.

In a few moments, she was back and leapt lightly from the wall. Scowling, she texted Bridget and refused to say a word till they were safely on the road again.

"Brand new kennel," Cori announced. "A large one, judging by the drainage setup."

Kinney accepted Leo back in her lap. "Okay, so we know where the puppies might end up, but we don't know where they are now."

"Onwards," Bridget said, pressing the pedal down hard. It felt—and sounded—like the old vehicle might fly apart, but that was nothing new. Kinney had often thought of the green van as the uncredited Mafia member that always drove getaway.

The next site was about 10 miles away, nestled into a

scenic little valley in a fold of the hills. This time, instead of getting too close, they drove up the range to a gravel viewing point, and used the binoculars. The second new kennel was a little behind the first in terms of development, and again, the house in front seemed uninhabited.

"Strike two," Evie said. "Let's hope we find the puppies at the last one."

Kinney nodded, but she doubted that would be the case. There was something bigger going on here. Clarence had been right. These sites were still the trees and they needed to zoom out to see the forest.

The last location had plenty of cover, so they parked well back and got out. This time, Evie joined Kinney and Cori as they got a closer look. There was a small bungalow fronting the kennel-in-progress.

"Another bust," Evie said. "Where are they stashing these missing but not-quite-stolen pups?"

"We'll find them," Kinney said. "For all we know they're at someone's house. It doesn't seem like there are many of them at the moment."

They were about to turn back when a blue pickup truck barreled down the lane toward them. Dodging into the bushes, they crouched to watch. The driver pulled up in front of the house, got out and started unloading supplies. He was wearing a baseball cap backwards, and red hair curled around it.

"Wowza," Evie said. "Cute, right? He looks familiar."

"It's the contractor who's been working at Runaway Farm," Kinney said. "I saw him at Leann Cosburn's place as well. He sure gets around."

"The hot ones always do," Evie sighed. "Although I've never fancied gingers. Being a ginger, and all. There'd be no surprises with the kids."

Kinney pulled her away. "Let's not ogle construction guys who are working on illicit kennels."

"These guys may not know they're illicit," Cori said. "Not that I'm condoning ogling." She continued to watch nonetheless. Turning to catch Kinney's eye she said, "What? I'm human. And single, last time I checked."

Evie shrugged as they walked back to the van. "They would have signed nondisclosure agreements for their plum government contract. Let Bridget set you up with someone better, Cori."

Cori rolled her eyes. "I take all that back. I'm not human after all."

CHAPTER SIXTEEN

The hills had been slow to green up that spring, but now, as June grew confident, vast stretches of long grass and wildflowers flanked the path in the hills above town. The 10 women stretched their legs and shook off the morning's adventure. Thoughtful as always, Remi pulled a container of cookies out of her backpack and passed them around. Then she offered apples.

For a while they munched in silence, digesting what they'd seen. The fresh air and sugar revived them before too long.

Duff stared around and sighed. "If it weren't for the hills, we probably would have given up on this place long ago. I couldn't handle the toxicity without coming here to recover."

Remi smiled as Leo raced after Beau. The tall black dog rarely left Bridget's side unless she commanded him to lighten up and run on the trails. Beau slowed to let Leo catch up and then sprinted off again. As they were often together on various adventures, the dogs had become old pals. At least, off duty. On duty, they ignored each other.

"That reminds me of when we brought Isla McInnis here

years ago," Remi said. "She said the air's like champagne. You sip and savor it."

"Who's Isla?" Evie asked. "The name sounds familiar."

"The brains behind Dog Town," Cori said. Her expression suggested the champagne had soured in her mouth. "She came here maybe eleven years ago to rescue a dog, and then wrote that famous article about how this is the best place for dogs and dog lovers in North America. It went to City Council's head like cheap bubbly and suddenly Dog Town was born."

"Isla meant well," Remi said. "She really loved it here. I was surprised she didn't move back."

"I think she was embarrassed over what happened to the city," Bridget said. "She dreamed of it becoming a fairy-tale destination, and the politicians turned it into a cartoon." She shrugged. "At least, that's what she said to me."

"You guys keep in touch?" Kinney asked. "I didn't know she was aware of what's happened here."

"She knows," Bridget said, with a grim smile. "I keep her posted whether she wants me to or not."

"I liked her." Remi stooped to pick some wildflowers. "We should get her back here to write another piece."

"I keep asking her to do an exposé, but she won't take the bait," Bridget said.

"Maybe puppy-gate will change her mind," Kinney said. "If we're right that the City is stealing puppies for a secret plan, it's big news—even if they made reparations."

Arianna had been quiet for most of the walk. Normally she was the embodiment of champagne—bubbly and upbeat. No doubt the mystery of the missing puppies weighed more heavily on a breeder than anyone else.

"Why on earth are they building large kennels?" she asked, at last. "When we were lobbying and consulting at

City Hall, it was all about keeping kennels small and numbers down. You practically had to promise your first child to get a permit to expand."

"Or promise your best puppy," Kinney said.

"But no one is even living in the houses that front these operations," Ari said. "Who exactly is benefiting?"

"That one's easy," Evie said. "The City is benefiting somehow. My first thought was that they were building facilities for government-run puppy mills. With the cream of the crop breeding stock."

Ari's bright cheeks paled and her mouth dropped open for a second. "Are you saying they're stealing our dogs to warehouse them at these sites?"

Evie shrugged. "Just guessing. Getting control of the Dog Town breeding brand would be quite a feat. I could see Mayor Bradshaw wanting to pick and choose the breeds that make Dog Town famous."

"Which explains why his lackeys wouldn't steal my downscale hybrids." Ari's wide blue eyes had narrowed to slits and though she still looked angelic, she seemed more likely to smite than bless. "If anyone takes one of my puppies, there will be hell to pay."

"Which is exactly why your dogs have been spared," Kinney said. "They know about your relationship with the Mafia. We have your back, you know that."

Ari couldn't force a smile. "I get queasy when I think of someone tampering with my puppies—and my bloodlines. Some may think breeding hybrids is random luck, but I invest tens of thousands each year to get the best breeding stock and then I test the heck out of them to make sure they're sound in health and temperament." Remi tried to hand Ari some flowers in lieu of the therapy beagle but Ari waved them away. "If they're intending to breed these stolen pups, they could make terrible mistakes with genetics."

"Sick puppies and heartbroken owners won't do much for the Dog Town brand," Kinney said. "That will backfire on Mayor Bradshaw."

"Agreed," Evie said. "If this is what he's up to, he's getting bad advice. Ill-informed advice."

Dropping the flowers, Remi started wringing her hands. "My heart hurts at the thought of these little puppies stuck in kennels without loving owners."

Kinney leaned down and caught Leo with both hands like a football as he shot past. He was still struggling as she passed him to Remi, but settled instantly when he was in her arms. Her eyes had filled with tears, but thanks to Leo, they didn't spill over.

Cori had been suspiciously silent through the debate, striding ahead but still in earshot. Finally she circled back. "It's all weird. The mayor is obviously up to something but he's fooled us before. I'm still mad about Runaway Farm."

"He's getting more slippery," Bridget said. "I think we need to observe very carefully before doing or saying anything."

"I don't want to watch and wait," Kinney said. "I want to throw a grenade and blow the plan up."

Everyone laughed, including Cori. "That sounds more like me," she said. "Usually you're all about stealth and proper pacing."

"I guess I'm just... what's the opposite of champagne?"

"Bitters," Cori said, smirking as she picked up a rock with gloved hands and hurled it down the rocky escarpment.

"That sounds about right. Here I am, basically fired, and I still have to take your Miracle Makeover Program and perform for City officials on July fourth."

Brushing dirt from her gloves, Cori turned. "And you'd better take that seriously. Yes, it's about protecting the dog from the City. But more importantly, it's about giving Whiskey his life back. He'll live in chronic anxiety if you don't create a safe bond and desensitize him to noise."

"I know, I'm not backing down. I just haven't seen much progress. The dog still only meets my eyes if I'm offering him a tennis ball. I aspire to mean more to him than that."

Bridget stared up the hill to where Beau stood on an outcropping, watching her. Her eyes softened with love and she smiled automatically. Kinney wondered if she ever looked that way at Sullivan, her boyfriend. It was easier to love a dog, at least in her experience. There were fewer complications—even when the complications were considerable. Despite their short time together, she already loved Whiskey. Not as much as she'd loved Kali, but enough that she wanted to help him be light and fun again, after his pain. Enough that she would be very upset if Jacinda Allen ever petitioned the City for his return. She'd half-expected Jacinda to track her down after Dan Barber surrendered Whiskey, but there'd been no word so far. Maybe the CCD had scared her off.

"Have you tried the umbilical cord?" Bridget asked.

"Excuse me?" Kinney's stomach was a little queasy and this didn't sound at all appealing.

Bridget smiled at her expression. "It's a training method, usually for little puppies. You leash the dog to you and they have to follow you everywhere, like it or not. It gets them used to you making the decisions."

Kinney looked at Cori, who nodded. "Worth a try. We're short on time for a dog who's been through so much change and trauma."

"Try agility," Ari said. "Or scent work. Any activity that

he might find fun when you're not doing drills. All work and no play makes for an unhappy dog."

"Or service dog classes," Evie suggested. "You never know what his calling might be."

Pushing strands of hair out of her eyes, Kinney laughed. "It's a good thing I have time on my hands."

Cori clapped her gloved hands. "I appreciate your enthusiasm for my canine client, folks, but that's too much too soon. Kinney just needs to socialize him well, expose him to noise gradually, and above all, act like she's queen of the world."

By this point, they'd reached the outcropping where Beau had stood. Kinney took his place, looking over the valley. Dorset Hills sat far below, cloaked in mist and looking more like a squat, dangerous toadstool than a bucolic town. She spread her arms and waved them. "I command thee to clean up thy act, Frog Town."

Everyone applauded and they laughed and joked all the way back down the trail, proving the truth of hillside magic. A menacing cloud might be threatening the future of their beloved town, but they could still enjoy fun and friendship today.

Kinney fell behind with Remi. "No advice from you about Whiskey? I want him to be like Leo, the happiest dog in the world."

"Leo's far from perfect," Remi said. "So my only advice is to bring Whiskey up here as much as you can. Champagne air is good for what ails any dog."

CHAPTER SEVENTEEN

K inney had only tripped and fallen twice since implementing the "umbilical cord" training approach Bridget had suggested in the hills a few days earlier. During nearly all their waking hours, Whiskey was hooked to a leash around her waist. He came everywhere with her, from the bathroom to running errands, with a few hours of crated quiet time during the day. Regular stints in his "cave" were part of good canine mental health, Cori said.

It felt odd to go to a meeting with a dog tied to her waist, but she'd cleared it first. An acquaintance of Marilyn Rossi had asked Kinney to give her advice on a dog security issue. She hadn't given much detail and Kinney hadn't pressed. She'd been working with Whiskey on his triggers as much as Cori's detailed program allowed, but that still left her with many hours to contemplate her suspension from work. She was torn between wanting to do something spectacular that would win her old job back, and finding a new path in life. Starting over wasn't as daunting as it had been when she left social work, but still... She'd expected to have her life on track by age 33. Here she was, practically couch surfing at Marti

Forrester's house, with no job and no real prospects. Her mind offered a constant stream of negative chatter that mostly sounded like her mother. So it was good to get out, no matter what.

"This is not what Mom wanted for me," she told Whiskey, as she pulled up in front of a large home in the upscale neighborhood of Farling Heights. The CCD still hadn't reclaimed the Prius, maybe because she still needed it for the Magical Makeover Program. No doubt they wanted to get full mileage out of that opportunity to humiliate her publicly. Hooking Whiskey up again after she parked, she continued her monologue as they walked up the long driveway. "Mom pictured me in some high-end, secure job with a reliable guy. And definitely a baby or two by now." She spun twice to release the leash wrapped around her waist, and realized it probably looked like a lighthearted whirl to anyone watching. "I can't even imagine what she'd say about the umbilical method."

Whiskey gave her a passing glance. While his eye contact was improving, he still wasn't offering the consistent gaze she craved. Clearly she wasn't worthy of his full attention yet, despite their constant contact.

Trina Belsky opened the double front doors before Kinney even knocked, and her hopeful smile cleared the cloud in Kinney's heart. Maybe she'd do some good today for someone in need. That's what had always driven her.

There was barking deep inside the house but Whiskey didn't talk back. He sat beside Kinney without being asked. "Why don't we just meet you around back?" Kinney said. "No point in tracking dirty paws through the house."

Trina nodded. "I'll leave Chester inside until you're ready for him." Her blue eyes, fine, fair hair and small build made her look like a china doll. Kinney would have expected her to choose a tiny lapdog rather than a large, powerful Rhodesian ridgeback.

Coming through the back gate, Kinney gasped. The yard was large and deep, and beautifully landscaped in a pet-resistant style. It looked like the work of Tiller Iverson, Remi's boyfriend. He was making a good living designing landscaping that could survive paws and jaws. People who could tailor their skills to Dog Town's unique needs tended to do very well here.

What really took her breath away was the large, custombuilt doggie "jungle gym." It had elements of an agility course and a kids' playground, and was made from a dogproof material. She'd never seen anything like it, but no doubt it would catch on quickly with those who could afford it.

"Wow," she said, as Trina came down the back stairs to join her. "Chester is one lucky dog."

"I wish he thought so," Trina said, her eyes filling instantly with tears. "He's got all this, but he still tries to escape constantly." She pointed to a newly built fence that was 10 feet tall. "That's higher than the City allows, but Chester got over." There were deep grooves in the wood at eye level. "He jumps, hooks his paws over the top and claws his way up. Sometimes he digs his way under, just for variety. We gave him this playground to work out his energy but I think it just enhanced his skills."

"How often does he make a run for it?" Kinney asked.

"Often enough that the neighbors complain. He's a friendly dog, but ridgebacks can be intimidating. Especially unneutered dogs." She patted her eyes. "It won't be long till someone calls the Tattletail hotline, and then... well, I don't even want to think about it."

"I assume you've seen a trainer and are doing all you can to give Chester enough structured exercise?"

She nodded. "We've seen a bunch, and I work with him constantly. He runs in the hills every day. The only option seems to be keeping him chained back here if we're not with him. But then he gets frustrated and destructive."

With Trina's permission, Kinney let Whiskey off the leash and he ran immediately to the jungle gym and climbed to the top platform. Then he slid down the doggie slide, ran through the tunnel, and started over.

Perching on the lowest platform, Kinney asked, "Do you mind if I ask why you contacted me? I'm not a trainer. In fact, I need a trainer myself with this guy."

"I know. I heard about what happened at the CCD and how you need to do that Miracle Makeover Program."

Kinney's face froze. She wasn't aware it was common knowledge, or that people would really be that interested in her life. "Yeah. All the more wonder why you called me."

Trina's eyes darted around anxiously, knowing she'd stepped in something. "I just thought that you could give us the CCD's perspective. Off the record."

"Doing things off the record is what got me benched," Kinney said. Watching Whiskey go down the slide again made her smile in spite of herself. "But I can say that you're right about what you fear. All it will take is one neighbor complaint about a big dog like Chester to get you a fine, if not more. Despite the fact that the City is trying to find a kinder, gentler approach, there's always going to be more worry about large dogs." She got up, called Whiskey and hooked him up again. "What I advise—on the record—is to get in touch with Cori Hogan. She's an amazing trainer, and the one offering the Miracle Makeover Program." She started towards the back gate. "Cori will get you on the right track, I'm sure of it."

"Wait!" Trina came after her and caught her sleeve. "I think— I think my husband's going to leave me over this. I heard you were good with..." She hesitated, finding the words. "Pet relationship problems."

Kinney turned back and saw a different kind of pain in Trina's eyes. "Well, I don't have a long track record, but I'm more than happy to listen. Maybe we'd better go inside for that."

Trina invited her into the kitchen and left her at the kitchen table while she went to let Chester out the side door into the yard. It was the most luxurious kitchen Kinney had ever seen. There was smooth marble and more than enough cupboards to fit everything she owned in life. She'd never accumulated much, however. Social work hadn't paid well and she felt guilty spending anything, when so many people were in more need. Opulence like this intimidated her, but people were people whether they lived in palaces or public housing, and nowhere did that show more than in relation to their pets. Dogs in particular were the great leveler. Even rich people had to pick up poop.

And even rich people had frantically high-energy dogs. Chester came around the side of the house like a rocket and ran right up the slide of his jungle gym. Before Trina even got back to the kitchen, he'd done a full circuit of all the activities and then run a fast lap around the yard, presumably looking for escape routes.

"Now that is a beautiful dog," Kinney said, when Trina came in. "Although he moves too fast to get a good look."

"That's my boy," Trina said, using a high-end coffeemaker to pull the best cup of coffee Kinney had ever smelled, let alone tasted. They sat at a heavy glass kitchen table, with Whiskey curled at her feet, ignoring Chester's clamor in the distance.

"Joey, my husband, has tried everything," Trina said. "The doggie playground was his idea and he's never complained about the cost of trainers or anything else. I think he might feel guilty because I wanted a dog I could carry around with me but he was embarrassed by froufrou dogs. Now the ridgeback *he* wanted is causing trouble—but I'm so in love with the dog that I could never even think about parting with him."

"It's a recipe for conflict, all right," Kinney said. "What's brought things to the breaking point now?"

"The neighbors complaining, I think," Trina said, getting up to pour two glasses of ice water for them. "He worries about people talking about us, whereas I worry about Chester getting hurt when he's gone."

"That's not all I care about," a male voice said.

Kinney turned and saw a tall, handsome man in the doorway. His brow was furrowed and his face flushed. He certainly didn't like his wife talking about their personal problems to strangers.

"Joey!" Trina jumped up and ran over to him. "I'm sorry. I know how this must sound."

"It sounds like you're oversharing," he grumbled, although he let her tow him to the table. "I don't understand."

Kinney half rose and shook his hand. "I'm Kinney, and this is my dog, Whiskey. He's tied to me because he has behavioral problems I'm trying to work out. I basically lost my job at the CCD because of him, so you're not alone in having a dog with challenges." She sat back down. "How's that for oversharing?"

Joey's hackles settled but he still looked confused. "Why exactly are you here, Kinney? You're obviously not a trainer."

"That's for sure. Trina thought I might be able to offer some insight from the City's perspective. But then we got to talking about how managing a difficult dog can stress you out and put pressure on relationships."

He nodded. "Yeah. Suddenly your whole world revolves around the dog. There's no room for anything else. It's not 'how was your day' anymore, but 'what did Chester do now?'"

Trina made him a coffee and he gave her a half smile as she slid it in front of him. "How was your day?" she asked, smiling.

"Good," he said. "It's always good till I get home."

Trina's smile faded as she sat down. "Is that how it feels?"

He stared down at his hands. "Not always. But lately."

"The fences are getting higher inside and out," Kinney suggested. "You don't feel heard."

"Sometimes it feels that way," he said. "If I show I'm upset, she gets so defensive about the dog. I don't know how to fix the problem."

Kinney looked at Trina. "You know that's what he's trying to do... fix the problem. So that you can go back to being a happy family again."

She nodded slowly. "But Chester's my baby."

Laughing, Kinney said, "That's why you need to see Cori Hogan. First thing she's going to tell you is that he's a dog, not a baby. A lot of us do that. It's actually doing Chester a disservice to treat him that way. The dog has some needs that aren't being met, and she'll tell you how to help. First thing she'll suggest is getting him neutered, of course. Then maybe flyball or agility or herding. I don't know. But there's a solution, I'm quite sure."

Both of them brightened. "I hope so," Joey said. "Because I want my happy wife back."

Trina reached out and grabbed his hand. "I'm still right here."

"It doesn't feel that way. You've been so withdrawn. It's like you're avoiding me."

"I'm just avoiding the arguing. When you're frustrated and angry I kind of shut down."

"I'm sorry," he said. "You can always talk to me. Just don't avoid me."

"When's the last time you had a vacation together? Just the two of you?" Kinney asked. "It would really help ease the stress."

"Since Chester," Joey said. "No boarding facility could hold him."

"I can hook you up with a good dog sitter," Kinney said. "She specializes in challenging dogs."

"That would go a long way," Joey said. "I'm just tired. My patience is short."

"I'd love it, too," Trina said. "I feel so guilty all the time. And scared. I'm worried you're going to make me give Chester up."

He shook his head. "I would never do that to you, Trina. Even when that guy offered me three times what the dog's worth, I didn't consider it for a second."

Trina's jaw just about hit the table. "Someone offered you money for Chester? Who?"

"I don't know. Just some guy. He called me at the office one day and offered me 10 grand for him."

"Did he *know* Chester? I mean, did he know what he was like?"

"He knew all about him. Said the neighbors had been gossiping. He told me he could take the dog off my hands and end the hassle."

Kinney wanted to question Joey herself but Trina was doing a fine job.

"I don't get it," Trina said. "Who would want him? I mean, he's the love of my life—aside from you—but even I can admit he's not a prize for someone else."

"I just gave him the brush-off and that was that. Selling him wasn't an option. I want my wife to be happy, no matter what."

They gazed at each other, and Kinney suspected only her presence was deterring a beautiful make up session. She cleared her throat and they jumped, as if they'd forgotten she was there. "Joey, do you have the number of this guy? I'd really like to speak to him."

"I deleted it. Why?"

"It's just a really weird and random thing, don't you think? When did this call happen?"

"Maybe two weeks ago." Joey downed the rest of his coffee. "Honestly, I wanted to put it out of my mind. I had this strange feeling he must be watching us."

Kinney stood up. "I don't want to worry you, but it's probably a good idea to keep Chester on leash for the next while. Just to be safe."

"You don't think someone would try to steal him?" Trina asked, clutching Joey's hand, her blue eyes wide with fear.

"We have security cameras, honey," he said.

"As long as he doesn't get out again, I'm sure you're fine," Kinney said. To lighten the mood, she added, "Besides, it's one thing to know about Chester and another to try to contain him."

They watched the dog doing another power cycle on the jungle gym, as if training for his big break. Suddenly Whiskey didn't seem like such a problem after all.

"Well, I'd better get going," she said. "Joey, please let me know if you remember anything more about this call. I just find it all so interesting."

She got to her feet and Whiskey stood, too, on his umbilical cord. As she turned, somehow the leash snagged her water glass and tipped it off the table. It hit the marble floor with a loud crash.

Whiskey flinched and started to shake but Kinney took a deep breath and turned to Trina and Joey. "Just ignore it, please. He's noise-sensitive and his trainer said that if something like this happened to act like nothing is wrong. It's business as usual, even if you broke a glass in someone's lovely kitchen."

They laughed and chatted for a few minutes before Trina calmly cleaned up the tinkling glass so they could safely cross the kitchen floor.

By the time they reached the front hall, Whiskey's tail was up and his tongue lolled in a happy smile. Similar smiles were on Trina and Joey's faces and she couldn't help smiling too, even though the stolen puppy plot had taken an unexpected turn.

"Good luck with Chester," she said, as they walked out to the porch. She scanned the street, but the only car passing was a grey Prius similar to her own. "I bet you're a huge success story in a few months. But take that vacation before the next phase, okay?"

"Done, Dr. Kinney," Trina said, hugging her. "But we'll be there to cheer you on at the Fourth of July festival, I promise. You and Whiskey are going to ace it."

Looking down at him, she saw he was looking up at her. His beautiful eyes didn't flick away for a good few seconds. "I hope so," she said. "Because he's turning into the new love of my life."

CHAPTER EIGHTEEN

Runaway Farm on a late June afternoon was balm to Kinney's soul. She'd grown up in Seattle, and never imagined enjoying small town life, let alone time on a farm. Yet she found herself heading out to lend Hannah a hand even more often now. Keeping the prankster goats out of trouble was better than a sitcom marathon for boosting her spirits. Besides, Whiskey was always welcome and could have a good run.

Hannah stood with her arms crossed over the fence, laughing as Kinney chased the two newest kids around. One had stolen her work glove, and goats were notorious for consuming non-consumables.

"How's it going with the missing puppy problem?" Hannah asked when Kinney returned to the fence, triumphantly waving the glove.

"We haven't caught much of a break yet," Kinney said. "After all the mysteries we've solved in Dog Town, this one's really stumping us." She hopped up on the fence. "Sadly, I think that's because it's bigger and deeper than all the rest."

Twisting long wavy hair into a messy bun, Hannah

sighed. "I wish I could be more help. I owe all of you so much. But this farm is kicking my butt."

Kinney spun around on the fence so she was facing the farm as it unfurled over glorious green fields. "It's going well, though, right?"

"Overall, yes. But there's always something going on." She reached over the fence and swatted a brown and white goat with her hat as it tried to get at Kinney's pant cuff through the slats. "Whether it's the animals or the contractors, there's not a second's downtime."

"And yet I've never seen you look happier," Kinney said. "Hard work agrees with you, princess."

Hannah swatted her with the hat, now. "How about you, my friend? Are you managing to stay happy, given all that's happened?"

"Up and down," Kinney admitted, leaping off the fence and landing lightly. "There's a lot of pressure with Cori's Miracle Makeover Program. I'm looking forward to the fourth like you would a stampeding pig."

"At least you'll have James helping you through it," Hannah said.

Kinney looked at her quickly. Hannah was grinning as she scanned the sheep pen for misbehavior.

"What's that supposed to mean?" Kinney asked.

Hannah's shoulders shrugged under the straps of her overalls. "I just hear about practice sessions in excruciating detail. The way he tells it, you're some kind of superhero, rescuing dogs in dangerous situations."

Heat rose quickly in Kinney's cheeks. "It's nothing the Mafia doesn't do every day. He hasn't seen Cori hanging from a zipline."

"I don't think it's Cori he wants to see." Hannah climbed another fence and moved among the sheep. She shoved some out of the way so the shyer sheep could get a chance at the hay. "It's Kinney-this and Kinney-that. Oh, and you have really nice hair, too." Hannah stroked a sweet lamb. "Someone's got a crush."

Now Kinney felt like the fence and the hay were at risk of catching fire from her flaming face. "I didn't realize it was quite like that. James must have a lineup of... normal women."

"Normal?" Hannah stood laughing among the sheep. "I don't even know what that is anymore. I can certainly say there's been no lineup of women since he came back to Dorset Hills. I'd know because he's still living here."

She was about to climb back over when Nick shouted from the barn. "There's a gate for a reason, Hannah."

Saluting him, she walked along the fence. "He'd like to roll me in bubble wrap, but it's really not feasible on a farm." Once she'd latched the pen behind her, she continued, "I haven't known you that long, Kinney, but I get the sense you're like me—a little slow to trust. All I'm going to say is that giving Nick a chance was my second smartest decision ever." She patted her slightly rounded belly. "Right after this."

"Point taken. And thank you," Kinney said, hoping to end the discussion. "Where is James, anyway? We're heading over to the Wolff County fair to expose the dogs to crowds, noise, and fireworks."

"With Alvina, if I had to guess. That's where I usually find him."

Sure enough, James was inside the pen with the fluffy brown alpaca. The two white llamas who kept Alvina company had moved to the other end in apparent disgust. The last time Kinney had seen them together, James had run up and down outside the pen while Alvina cavorted and high kicked inside. It seemed that their relationship had progressed nicely. Today they were actually playing tag around an obstacle course of barrels and benches. He took a running leap onto a picnic table and leapt off the other side, only to find Alvina in front of him spinning in circles. Laughing, he took off again, and then stopped dead when he saw the women at the fence.

"Hey," he said, while Alvina nibbled at his hair and collar. "You're early."

"Didn't want to miss the show," Kinney said, grinning.

He jumped the fence easily. "It's a good workout. I'll grab a shower and be back in five."

"Isn't it amazing that guys can grab a shower and be ready in five?" Kinney said. "It took me nearly an hour to get ready, and it's only a county fair."

"Farm life pares down your routine," Hannah said, giving her a sideways glance. "But you look nice."

"I feel pressure to keep myself up after Sasha's makeover," she said, following Hannah to the farmhouse. Half a dozen guys were working on a large addition on one side. "I've seen that tall, redheaded guy around."

"Tanner Glenn? Yeah. He has projects around town. He's known for high-end craftsmanship. Sullivan Shaw recommended him." She eyed Kinney again. "You cheating on my brother already?"

"No! I mean, I don't even think that guy's cute."

"Oh, he's cute all right," Hannah said, laughing. "Now I'm surrounded by cute all day and I'm out of commission anyway."

James came out looking fresh and handsome, in jeans, a white T-shirt and denim jacket. He was surprisingly adaptable, going from suits to country causal without missing a beat. His personality was like that too—good with anyone, and always accommodating. It seemed effortless, whereas Kinney had to work hard to be social. Then she had to refill her tank in the hills or out here on the farm.

There was little need for chitchat on the way to the Wolff County fair, and once there, they both needed to focus 100 percent on their dogs. Whiskey was on a regular leash, weaving through the crowd, and sometimes falling behind to nudge her in the right direction, like a true herding dog. There were plenty of loud noises, and she made sure to keep her shoulders back, her eyes up and her arms loose. He managed the deafening games area like a champ, even with all the ding-ding-ding of prizewinners.

James and Rocky were doing well, too. Luckily, the tripe was no longer needed and the big dog parted the crowd confidently. People naturally fell back to stare, and while Rocky didn't welcome the attention, he didn't avoid it, either. He was basically indifferent, which was about as good as it was likely to get given his breed traits.

They reached the other end of the fairground and found a quiet place on a hill to rest. The dogs lolled on the grass, comfortable now in each other's company. Kinney and James split a huge pastrami sandwich and sipped soda.

"What now?" James asked, around a mouthful. "Do we need to repeat?"

"I think we're good." She chewed thoughtfully and swallowed before saying, "Would you mind going on a little mission with me?"

"Sure," he said. "As long as you fill me in first. I never know what to expect with you."

"It's just a drive-by," she said. "I heard about a building project over here in Wolff County that Dorset Hills is funding."

He tipped his head. "That sounds odd."

"It does, indeed. I have my suspicions about what it might be, and while we're here, I figured we'd check it out."

Crunching on potato chips, he asked, "What do you think it is?"

She eyed him, wondering whether or not to be honest. Finally she took the leap. "I think it's an illicit dog kennel for stolen puppies."

James gasped, inhaling some potato chip crumbs and spraying others around when he coughed. "Pardon me?"

She gave him the broad brushstrokes of what they already knew about the puppy situation.

"This is all confidential, of course." She ate the last bite of her sandwich and swallowed, finding it had turned to sawdust. "I trust you."

He brushed potato chip crumbs from his shirt and Whiskey came over to help with the cleanup, snuffling loudly. "Do you think the mayor's aware of all this?"

"He knew about the first missing puppies, so yes. Besides, there's a ton of money invested in these kennels. I don't know if it's taxpayers' dollars or his own private sources. Either way, someone is backing this in a big way." Taking the straw out of the soda, she downed half of it and then hiccupped. "All that I can find is vague records with no details. And who knows what else isn't even listed?"

Brow furrowing, he stared at her. "How are you finding all this out? I thought you were on suspension."

Now she hesitated. James was an honorable guy and her techniques might very well put him off. But since she didn't plan to stop doing what she considered the right thing, she might as well be honest. If it pushed him away, so be it. He needed to know the worst.

"Snooping," she said at last. "I found a back door into the CCD system."

"A back door?" His eyebrows had soared and his blue eyes were laser sharp.

"A password, to be more precise."

James waited for an explanation and when it didn't come, he pressed, "And how exactly did *that* fall into your hands?"

"Old fashioned legwork. I have time on my hands now, so I followed CCD employees to the park and observed. You'd be surprised how many people use their dog's name as their password." She grinned at him. "It was easier than I expected."

James blinked a few times, flashing blue on and off. "Are you saying you essentially hacked into the system and poked around till you found this property purchase in the City's name?"

She picked through the grass looking for a four-leaf clover. "I'm not proud of it." Pulling out a few, she examined them and then let them drop. "Well, maybe I am. A little. Technically I'm still on staff, I guess."

"Huh." James ran his hands over Rocky's fluffy coat, apparently digesting everything. She kept picking clover, waiting for his verdict. The longer he was silent, the faster her fingers plucked at the grass.

Finally she couldn't stand the suspense. "I'm sure our Mafia strategies come as a bit of a shock."

He nodded and then shrugged. "Mayor Bradshaw was completely underhanded in his dealings with Hannah, so I guess it shouldn't surprise me that he's up to no good in other ways. Do you think there's deep corruption in City Hall?"

"Yeah, although we don't know the full extent of it. This is the biggest issue we've discovered. If we can get proof, Evie thinks it may be enough to oust the mayor." She double-knotted her sneakers. "More importantly, we need to find the pups that are still MIA."

James stuffed the rest of his sandwich back into the bag, uneaten. "I've lost my appetite." He stared down at the fairground, filled with happy families enjoying the beautiful day. "I thought country life would be... sweeter."

"It's still sweet," she said, smiling. "You just need to know where to bite."

He got to his feet and offered his hand. "Okay, let's go sniff out some political rot." Picking up the trash and Rocky's leash, he added, "It can't be worse than tripe."

"Sadly, there are worse smells than tripe and the mayor is behind some of them."

James didn't say much as he drove the 10 miles to the site Kinney had identified. She left him in peace, feeling sad about destroying his beliefs about his hometown. She'd had years to adapt to the political waters heating up and barely noticed she was boiling. For James, it was pretty much instant scalding. He really wanted to see the best in everyone and everything and she liked that about him. Hopefully that quality wouldn't be totally crushed in the jaws of Dog Town.

The address led them to an old farmhouse with half a dozen large outbuildings. From a distance, it looked abandoned and even derelict. Unlike the other sites, there were no obvious signs of renovation.

"Looks like this lead's a bust," James said, as she peered out the window with binoculars.

"Not necessarily." She handed him the binoculars. "Look way back on the property. There are a dozen big trash bins and they're all full."

"That doesn't make sense," he said, raising the binoculars. "The place looks abandoned."

She took the binoculars back and stared a little longer. Finally she nodded. "I see a pink and white bag sticking out of the fullest bin. Unless I'm much mistaken, it's from Dr. Barkley's Organic Puppy Food."

James took another look while she searched for the brand on her phone. She showed him the dog food and he nodded. "Looks like it."

"I think one of those outbuildings is now a kennel," she said, scanning repeatedly, hoping to pinpoint which one.

"Do you want to go closer?" he asked. "We can walk down there and take a look."

"No." She lowered the binoculars, feeling red rings around her eyes from pressing too hard. "I mean yes, I sure do. But if you look above the light on the largest building in the middle, you'll see a security camera. Where there's one, there's more."

James looked again. "The City's getting smarter."

She nodded. "Which means we need to get smarter, too. For once, I'm going to stand down and ponder before acting. I'm trying to retrain myself. I can be too quick off the draw sometimes."

He laughed. "Ya think?"

Slapping his arm lightly, she said, "Drive. Find us a nice spot to watch the fireworks and traumatize my dog."

There was a little park on a hill just high enough to offer a fantastic view of the Wolff County fairgrounds. The place was empty now that darkness had fallen, so all the picnic tables were vacant. James found two old blankets in the back of his SUV. He spread one over the table with the best view. When they were settled, he draped the other around their shoulders. On his right, Rocky gave a heavy sigh and lay down on his side on the stony ground. Whiskey was alert on her left, ears forward as he sniffed the air. She unbuckled her belt and looped his leash through it. If he tried to take off, he'd have to drag her along. There was no way she'd risk losing him if he bolted into the night.

As they waited for the fireworks to start, Kinney felt a nervous prickling inside. She didn't know if it was worry about Whiskey, or proximity to James. Warmth was seeping around her and somehow pulling her closer. With a great effort, she pulled herself away. She couldn't afford to get lulled into a trance by James' magnetism. Without the helpful reek of tripe, she couldn't miss his woodsy scent. There was nothing strange or exotic about that smell. It was seductively simple and comforting. She realized in a flash that she'd needed comforting for a very long time. But tonight, she needed to stay alert. This was not the time to float away on fluffy cedar clouds.

"Why a Tibetan mastiff?" she asked suddenly.

James sat up a little straighter, perhaps shaking off the same spell. "I'm not sure. I liked the look—the big fluffy bear. But I think it was more their self-possession. I visited a couple of breeders and the dogs just seemed full of quiet confidence. Like they know their place in the world and are happy with it."

"That's exactly what I see in Rocky, especially now that he's settling in. It makes sense that he needed more security and routine. His breed probably likes predictability." She looked down at the splayed-out dog. "He did so well today. You must be proud."

James nodded, pulling the blanket a little closer and bringing her with it. "I want him to be happy. Now it feels like things are falling into place."

He slipped his arm around Kinney under the blanket and she fell into place, too. It seemed like a natural fit, like that missing piece of a puzzle. This time she didn't resist.

The first explosion made them all jump. Well, all except

Rocky, who didn't move a muscle. Whiskey was on his feet, and his mouth opened in an anxious pant.

Kinney took a deep breath and... did nothing. She didn't say a word to calm him or even move from her spot. Instead, she took slow, easy breaths, knowing he could sense her calm. A bright shower of color appeared overhead and while she looked down, Whiskey looked up. She could see blue and red reflected in his eyes. But his tail came up gradually to its normal relaxed position. His mouth closed. And ultimately, he sat. Still alert, but calm.

The next explosion, he looked up at her and she met his eyes, smiling. "All good, buddy."

Staring up again at the shower of sparkling lights, she turned back to James. "Are they making fireworks bigger these days?" she asked. "They were never like this when I was a kid. And of course they're rarely allowed in Dog Town out of respect to the dogs."

James shrugged. "These are pretty tame compared to New York City." He turned and grinned at her, his eyes still bright in the sparkling light. "But I like them better here."

She grinned back at him. "Oh yeah? Are they sweeter?"

"Let me get back to you on that." Pulling her even closer, he leaned down and kissed her. She opened her eyes for just a second and saw bursts of fireworks all around him—explosions of red, white, blue and even green. When he pulled away, he said, "Yeah. Definitely sweet."

"Like champagne," she said. "It really goes to your head."

"But no hangover," he said. "And it's safe to drive."

Laughing, she let his warmth pull her even closer. "Be sure to kiss responsibly."

CHAPTER NINETEEN

The sun forced its way through the trees only to glance off the bronze chow chow and dazzle Kinney's eyes. It reminded her of the fireworks the night before and her face suddenly warmed. She looked down at Whiskey, tied to her belt, and then pinched her arm. There was a time for kissing and a time for business. In fact, there was really no time for kissing right now, and the sooner she pushed that to the back of her mind the better.

"Kinney, it looks like you're getting sunburned," Evie said, raising her camera. "You should be wearing a hat."

Cori sized Kinney up and then turned to Evie. "What are you doing here, and with a camera no less? Who invited Evie?"

"I did," Bridget said, leaning against the chow chow. "We need political insights, Cori. Evie's more than proven her loyalties."

"Well, put down the camera." Cori paced with her gloved hands balled into fists. "Mafia meetings used to be top secret, just the core five. Now it's a free-for-all. That's no way to run a vigilante group."

Bridget continued to give Cori the calm smile that usually soothed the tiny trainer's jangled spirits. "The group has grown because the problems in Dorset Hills have grown. No one has joined us without being thoroughly checked out." She pushed off the chow and faced Cori. "I think we've been incredibly lucky to gather so many like-minded women to share our load."

Cori grunted, but her fingers gradually unfurled till the orange flares showed again. "We need to have confidentiality agreements or something."

"Well, I trust everyone here to use her judgement," Bridget said looking around.

The small clearing was pretty much full. Remi, Sasha and Evie sat on the base of the statue, while Duff, Ari, Maisie, and Nika perched on an old log on the other side. Mim, Hannah, and Flynn Strathmore, the artist, had also made their first appearance at a chow chow Rescue 911 meeting. Kinney had been in and out for years, but it was true this was the largest attendance they'd ever had. Unlike Cori, she felt buoyed. Working in the CCD, she'd often felt lonely and isolated. Now she felt well-supported in her efforts to do the right thing for pets in Dog Town.

"I wouldn't mind so much if it weren't here at the chow chow," Cori grumbled. "This place is almost sacred."

Kinney pushed herself off the trunk of a huge oak tree. "Would it help to know I did full background checks on everyone here?"

There was a ripple of protest throughout the crowd. "You didn't," Evie said.

"Of course I did. That's what I do. We need to rely on each other, and I don't like surprises any more than Cori does."

Cori reached over and gave Kinney a gloved high five. "Yeah, it does help. Can I get a copy of their files?"

Kinney laughed and shook her head. "Classified, but I will tell you about some information I hacked out of the CCD technology system yesterday."

She shared the story of finding the disguised kennel in Wolff County. "We didn't go near it because of security cameras. I needed to brainstorm with you guys first."

"Who's 'we'?" Cori asked, eyes narrowing.

"James and I," Kinney said. "We were at the Wolff County fair desensitizing the dogs so I figured we could take a look."

Cori planted her hands on her hips, orange flares prominent. "You decided to share this with James Pemberton first, instead of us?"

"Like I said, we were already there." Kinney crossed her arms against Cori. "Are you questioning my loyalty? Because I will share *my* file with you. My rescue credentials match yours."

Cori crossed her arms, too. "No way, no how."

"Kinney. Cori. Settle." Bridget came toward them. "Everyone's getting edgy with the stakes rising."

"She shouldn't be blathering to James," Cori said. "He's a big question mark."

"Not to me," Kinney said.

"All of us share with our partners from time to time," Bridget said. "And all of us hold things back when we need to. That system has been working fine. We understand the meaning of discretion."

"He's not her partner," Cori said. "He's just some rich guy I paired her up with in the Miracle Makeover Program."

"That rich guy happens to be my brother." Hannah's

voice was light but she added, "And I notice you have no problem using my farm for Mafia purposes."

"That's enough, Cori," Bridget said. "It's hard to see things change, but if there's anything we've learned in our years together, it's how to adapt."

Raising her camera, Evie tried to lighten the mood. "Maybe Bridget isn't the only matchmaker in our circle," she said, grinning. "Because I think that Wolff County fair outing was a date."

Kinney glared at her. "What I want to know is how the 911 meeting I called turned into a debate about my loyalties."

"And your love life," Evie added.

Kinney turned her glare on Cori. "You're the one in bed with the City with your training program. Maybe you're losing your objectivity."

"I can play both sides just fine," Cori said. Her hands were fisted again and her face flushed, too. Kinney didn't remember seeing that happen before.

"People, people." Remi got up from the base of the statue. "You're upsetting Leo. He wants to help but he doesn't know which one of you to choose."

Kinney stretched out her arms. "I'll take him. I could use a big dose of beagle."

Bridget clapped. "Look, all of us are nervous. Maybe this problem feels bigger than we can handle. But I'm quite sure we can figure it out... working together." Turning to Kinney, she said, "I called the 911. I didn't realize you had, too."

"You did? Why? What's happened?"

"This morning I paid my usual visit to Animal Services to see whether any dogs had come in. Like you know, I adopt as many dogs as I can to foster or rehabilitate them myself. The staff give me first dibs because they know I can do a better job of placing them than they can. It makes them look good. Our little system works and no one's complained so far."

"What changed today?" Kinney asked.

Bridget took a deep breath. "When I arrived there was the most gorgeous bearded collie pup you've ever seen. Looked like a purebred. Naturally I tried to snap him up, but the staff said he was 'on reserve.' No matter how hard I pressed, they wouldn't say more."

"You think he's targeted for the City's puppy project," Kinney said.

"Well, something is off. I know these people well and they were definitely acting guilty."

Cori's hands relaxed again and she said, "Can we steal the puppy before someone else does?"

"Not easily. They moved him to a back room to get him away from me."

"That means someone else is coming to pick him up," Cori said. "We've got to do something."

Kinney put Leo back in Remi's arms. "I've got an idea. Bridget, you're with me. We've got to make a stop at my place, first." She glanced back at the clearing as she left. "Stand by, everyone. If all goes well, we'll deploy later today and it'll take the full team."

"I DON'T THINK this will work," Bridget muttered, leading Kinney into the Animal Services building on the outskirts of Dorset Hills.

"It won't if you get jittery," Kinney said. "Calm down and act like this is life and death for this puppy. For all we know, it might be."

Bridget took a deep breath and plastered on a smile.

"Hey, guys," she called, walking into the adoption area. "I hope you don't mind but I brought a friend to meet the bearded collie pup. She's never seen one before."

A tall, bearded man looked Kinney up and down. "I know you."

She gave him a bland smile. "I don't think we've met. I've been told I look like every girl next door."

"No, I've definitely seen you... on TV. Aren't you the one who crawled into that culvert on Craven Road to save the Jack Russell?"

"Ah, yes," Kinney said, smiling for real. "That was me. Stinky awful rescue with a dead possum up the pipe. I bet you've done even worse."

"A few times, I guess. Yeah." Looking back at Bridget, he said, "We're under orders to keep the puppy quarantined. But I'll give you five minutes. For the rescue hero, here."

Kinney reached out and shook his hand. "Thank you so much. We rescuers need to stick together."

They sat in the small visitation room intended for prospective adopters to meet available dogs. When the bearded attendant brought in the puppy, Kinney squealed and held out her arms. At the same moment, Bridget rose and followed the man out, trying to convince him once more to let her adopt the dog. "I have the perfect home for her, Tom. I don't see why you won't let me take her."

While they argued, Kinney examined the squirming pup up and down. Before long, Bridget had annoyed Tom enough that he came back to collect the pup. "It's out of my hands. Seriously. I could lose my job."

"But she's perfect." Bridget hugged the puppy. "It's not often I fall so hard for a dog, you know that. Will you at least let me give her a pretty collar? So the new owners will know she was loved?"

He shook his head. "Whatever. It's not like you to be so... girly."

"Newsflash, I am a girl. And I know for a fact that you fall for some dogs more than others, too."

He nodded grudgingly and stepped out again.

Kinney took a faux diamond collar out of her pocket and put it on the pup. "Let's call her Bling, because she looks like a little princess now." Her voice quavered a bit. "I hope whatever comes next doesn't traumatize her, and she gets to have the great life she deserves."

Squeezing Kinney's free hand, Bridget nodded. "Me, too. I feel terrible sending her into the unknown. If we could just run for it—"

"Two of us couldn't take down Tom. Plus, they'd only grab her back and sideline us." She sighed. "Right now, this seems like our best chance to get to the heart of the problem."

"I guess." Bridget looked more discouraged than Kinney had ever seen her. She needed Beau badly.

On the way out, Kinney shook Tom's hand again. "You guys do great work in sometimes thankless circumstances. I salute you."

Back in the Prius, she checked her phone. "Operational," she said. "As long as they don't take that collar off, we can track our little Bling."

They pulled away and parked well out of sight. Soon, other Mafia cars took their stations all around the building. Someone was likely to come before too long to collect the puppy from one of the many entrances. There was no telling where they'd deliver little Bling, but they were ready to follow.

Hours passed and Kinney began wondering if she'd been wrong, or if they'd removed the pretty collar. She hoped that practically burying it in the pup's fluffy fur would make it unnoticeable to the person who claimed her. The signal from the tracker flashed steadily from inside the building, so the collar itself was still there.

Bridget had nodded off with her head against the passenger door of the Prius by the time the signal began moving. At first Kinney thought she was imagining it. Dusk had fallen and lights were coming on around them. Holding the phone up to her nose, she confirmed it. Then she texted the others: "Bling's on the move."

Gently touching Bridget's shoulder, she said, "It's go-time."

She was awake in an instant. "Really? I can't believe it worked!"

"All we know is that the collar itself is moving. But I can't see why anyone would carry that around on its own. I wish there'd been another way to plant a tracker on the pup, but the technology isn't there yet."

A van pulled out of the loading bay at the side of the Animal Services building. Trucks and vans had been coming and going all day and there was nothing to set this one apart. It was white without identifying markings. But at least white was visible in the dusk.

She handed her phone to Bridget to track the signal and keep everyone posted. They set off in a well-spaced convoy of four sedans. They'd used the vehicles least likely to attract notice.

Kinney went first, keeping far enough back to avoid notice—automatically speeding up and slowing down in pace with the van.

"I get the feeling you've tailed a good few people before," Bridget said.

"Yep, and I continued to practice so I wouldn't get flustered when a real need comes along."

"I've never seen you flustered on a 911," Bridget said. "You're always cool as a cucumber."

"Not so. I'm like a duck floating along the surface. Down below, everything's churning like crazy."

"I try to be a duck, too," Bridget said. "Beau's a big help with that. I hope Whiskey brings you the same peace one day."

"Me too," Kinney said. "But don't get me talking about Whiskey or I'll lose sight of the van."

They passed one of the many bronze Labrador retrievers that sat sentinel at the city border and kept going, out past Runaway Farm.

An odd feeling percolated in Kinney's abdomen. It was either intuition, or a bad memory surfacing to warn her. She kept the feeling to herself. There was nothing concrete and no reason to worry the team.

"We're in Wolff County," Bridget said. "The site you visited with James must be their destination."

"Possibly. They seem to have a lot of places locked down."

The percolating feeling grew until she actually felt nauseated. This wasn't typical nerves, because she did scary things all the time. Something was wrong. Very wrong. And she couldn't figure out what.

"He's turning off," Bridget said, pointing.

There was just a second's hesitation at the entrance before the van proceeded down the long lane that led to the property she'd seen with James the day before. Kinney pulled over and waited for the others to catch up.

"Text everyone that we're going up the hill," she said. "There's a viewing platform where you can see the full property."

They convoyed up the hill, with the lights turned off, and

then parked and got out of the car. Everyone had dressed warmly, because nights were chilly in the hills. Several of them had binoculars, and Evie had a telephoto lens, but they'd be of little use without more light. All they had was a single streetlamp some distance away.

Kinney stared through her binoculars in silence as the van backed up to the outbuilding she'd suspected of being renovated. The headlights went off and there was the sound of a door slamming. At this rate, they wouldn't be able to see a thing. But then floodlights came on and everything was clear as day.

"What are they doing?" Mim said, clutching Ari's arm. "Can you see anything?"

"A guy's getting out of the van and opening the side door. He's pulling something out. It's a—"

"Portable dog carrier," Cori supplied. "He's got the puppy."

"Make that two puppies," Kinney said, as he stacked one crate on top of the other.

They watched as the man pressed a code into a security panel on the wall and then used a key to unlock the door. He shouldered it open so that he could carry both crates inside at once.

Up on the hill, it seemed like they collectively held their breath. No one made a peep until the man emerged empty-handed.

"Oh my," Kinney said, leaning forward as if that would help her get a closer look. "I know that guy. It's Wyatt Cobb."

Bridget grabbed her jacket and pulled her back. "Who's Wyatt Cobb?"

"The newest dog cop at the CCD. He seemed like a nice enough guy. I guess they got to him."

"Well, what do we do now?" Ari said. "We know the

bearded collie pup and at least one other dog is in there. Who knows how many more?"

Cori shrugged. "Easy. We need to break in."

"Not that easy," Bridget said. "It's a secure site."

"We've gotten inside secure buildings before," Cori said. "Even Animal Services, to save Fritz, remember?"

"Oh yes, I remember. But we had someone inside helping us. Kinney, what do you think? Any way we could get this Cobb onside?"

Kinney lowered her binoculars and turned to them. She tried to speak but her mouth had dried suddenly and nothing came out.

"What?" Evie said, touching her arm. "You look like you've seen a ghost."

"Worse," Kinney said. "Wyatt stopped before he got in the van and looked up here. And then he smiled right at us."

"What?" Evie was alarmed. "Why would he do that? Our lights are out and there's no way he'd see us. How could he know?"

The van pulled out, and just before he left the lot, Wyatt flashed his headlights twice. Saying goodbye.

"Because we've been played," Kinney said. "My spidey sense was tingling most of the way here. Now I realize he was pausing slightly just often enough to make sure we were still behind him."

"Does this mean the puppy isn't really there?" Remi asked, clutching Leo close.

"Not necessarily. But it means they led us here for a reason."

Cori let her binoculars dangle and rubbed her face with one gloved hand. "They baited us out."

"Exactly," Kinney said. "I mean, look at us. We're almost all here. They could take the entire Mafia down in one fell swoop. We'd get arrested for breaking and entering. Maybe worse."

"What's worse than that?" Remi asked.

"Fines," Kinney said. "I know I can't afford that. We'd have a record, which would affect our employment. At worst —and I really wouldn't put it past them—they could seize our dogs."

"What? How?" Cori said.

"It's in regulation," Kinney said. "If someone has a criminal record, the CCD can seize a dog if there's the slightest concern about its welfare. Of course, that would be entirely at CCD discretion. I certainly don't want Wyatt Cobb using his discretion about Whiskey."

There was a moment of silence, as if someone had passed away. Their rebel spirit, possibly. Kinney knew that none of them could risk losing her own dog unless success was a sure thing. And this was far from a sure thing.

"So then what do we do?" Remi asked, at last.

"The only thing we can do," Kinney said. "Disappoint them."

"Agreed," Bridget said. "We leave, regroup and then try something else."

Cori's boots crunched on gravel as she paced. Now she stopped and turned. Kinney expected outrage, but Cori surprised her. "We lost this battle. They got us good. But that doesn't mean we've lost the war. We'll prevail, as always."

She stretched out a gloved hand and one by one the women set their hands on top of hers. They gave a quiet cheer and then dispersed into the night.

CHAPTER TWENTY

"Gorgeous," Evie said, stepping back to admire Kinney. She'd just finished applying makeup with a deft hand, at the same time as Sasha was doing a blowout on Kinney's hair. While she was painting and plucking, Evie lectured Kinney on how to behave at the mayor's formal reception to celebrate voluntarism in Dorset Hills. Kinney had been invited for her longstanding work on the board of a kids' drop-in center. James was her date—not because she'd invited him, but because Cori had decided the event was the perfect dress rehearsal for the Fourth of July festival and dog obedience test, now just days away. It was a Miracle Makeover assignment, and Kinney was the one getting made over. Again. For a few seconds, she longed for her tan CCD uniform but that quickly passed. It was unlikely she'd ever wear it again, and that was for the best.

Marti Forrester's little house was filled with laughing women offering advice on everything from clothing and shoes to clever one-liners. Kinney tried to absorb it all, but her main focus was Cori, who literally blocked the mirror so that every twitch of her orange fingers would be noticed.

"Don't take your attention off Whiskey for one second," she said. "This type of event has potential for every single one of his triggers: loud noises, sudden movements, and raised voices. All you need to do is move slowly through the crowd with a relaxed grip on his leash, speak calmly to different people, and above all, stay cool if there's unexpected noise. In fact, expect unexpected noise and stay cool the whole the time."

"And don't fall off your shoes," Evie added, dangling a pair of high-heeled sandals that belonged to Duff, whose feet happened to be the same size as Kinney's.

"Or out of your dress," Sasha said, holding up a sleek sapphire number that plunged in the front. "It's a little small, but don't worry, we'll tape it."

"Are you kidding me?" Kinney said. "How can I focus on Whiskey or the mayor if I'm worried about falling out of my dress?"

"I wouldn't worry about the dress," Evie said. "You'd recover from exposing yourself but not from losing control of the dog. Besides, if people are staring at your décolletage they're less likely to notice any missteps by the dog."

Cori clapped gloved hands. "There won't be any missteps by the dog. He's doing very well. All you need to do is be hyper-attuned to your surroundings. That's your forte anyway."

Kinney nodded. That had always been a strength. But there were so many other things to tune into as well.

"When you've got the mayor alone, see if you can find out anything about the puppies," Bridget said.

"Like he'd just spill that," Cori said.

"You'd be surprised at what he'll say sometimes," Evie said. "He's a complicated mix of sly and stupid. It's easier dealing with just one or the other."

"Well, first I have to get his attention," Kinney said. "He never seems to know me."

"That's what the dress is for," Evie said. "Plus, it's his job to talk to everyone being honored at the reception. Once you've got him cornered, start with something unexpected."

"My plan is to talk about Clarence Dayton," Kinney said, getting up from the hair and makeup station at the kitchen table and moving into the living room for wardrobe. "His office never followed through on their agreement to discuss the Dayton estate."

Evie winced. "You might be taking on too much for one short event."

"Well, I can't dive right into a chat about missing puppies and Mafia traps. So I might as well try that first."

"Don't chase him off," Bridget said. "You could try chitchat about rare breeds in Dog Town. See if he spills anything about his dastardly scheme."

Blowing out a long breath, Kinney slipped into the tight dress and permitted herself to be taped up.

"It's also a hot date," Remi said, smiling. "Remember to have fun."

"Impossible. This is a bigger ordeal than the Fourth of July event. That I won't need to do in heels and half a dress."

Cori grinned. "Didn't I mention the exam is black tie, too?"

"I'm not laughing," Kinney said. "Mostly because I can't breathe."

"Think of it as a game," Remi said. "Just do your best to overcome all the obstacles in 90 minutes." She tried to offer Leo, but Kinney shook her head. Whiskey's long guard hairs had found their way onto the blue dress already.

"Don't forget about Rocky," Cori said. "This will be an even bigger challenge for him, since he doesn't like crowds or strangers being too familiar. Keep an eye on his posture and demeanor, and tell James to take a breather outside on the patio if the dog's getting overstimulated. You two need to look out for each other."

"Got it." Kinney let Duff arrange a shawl over her shoulders. She'd never quite seen the point of a shawl. A cardigan was a more sensible choice. Turning to Cori, she said, "A rescue raid would be so much easier, you know? I'd rather squeeze through a culvert."

"Right? Better you than me, girl." Cori offered a rare pat on Kinney's shoulder. "Kick ass and take names. Bonus points if you stab the mayor with those shoes."

JAMES' eyes widened when she walked down the front steps. "Wow. You look amazing. The Cinderella of dog cops."

That made her smile. She felt desperately uncomfortable but James knew how to offer a compliment that wouldn't make her feel more self-conscious. He looked as handsome and comfortable in his tuxedo as he did in jeans, but she definitely preferred him casual.

"It's just a costume," she said, taking his hand for the last steps. "To help us get the job done."

"You wear it well." He let Whiskey into the back of the SUV, and then helped her into the front seat. "I wish I had a pumpkin to transform into a nice ride."

"I'm not one for fancy coaches," Kinney said, after he got behind the wheel. "My family is working class, and barely that. When I moved here I was happy to get away from people's perceptions. Dorset Hills was a different town, then. Nobody judged."

James drove down the road past the new bronze Pomeranian in the parkette on the corner, and headed for the city core. "I've never seen a more classless place than Dorset Hills," he said. Then he laughed. "I guess I mean class-conscious. Money and family don't seem to matter much here. What brings status is the dog you own, how you serve dogs, and most importantly, how you support the City brand."

"Interesting," Kinney said. "I hadn't really thought about it that way. Of course, I have a problem dog, serve other dogs by nefarious means, and undercut the mayor whenever possible. So I guess I don't have much class by the new definition either."

James reached over and squeezed her hand. "You are plenty classy by any standard, Kinney Butterfield."

Heat tingled in her hand and seared up her arm. She tried to ignore it. That kind of thing could derail a mission. She needed all her focus and then some. But her eyes kept drifting down to his hand, resting on top of hers on her knee. His fingers felt rough, as if he'd built some calluses working on the farm. He wasn't the same guy who arrived in Dorset Hills, either.

To distract herself, she filled him in on what Cori had said about the dogs.

"I am worried about Rocky," James said. "It's one thing to mingle with a crowd outdoors at a fair. It's another to be trapped in a room with other dogs. There's no room for escape."

"Evie said the reception room has a patio. We can escape out there to give the dogs a breather."

"Sounds like a plan," he said, pulling into the public parking lot outside Bellington Square. He gave her hand another squeeze. "We're going to rock this dress rehearsal."

She smiled up at him. "And the exam. In a week, we're home free."

Inside, everyone was circling Mayor Bradshaw like well-dressed turkey vultures, waiting for an opportunity to swoop in for a political snack. She wondered how she'd penetrate that crowd even to start a conversation, let alone cover all the ground she'd planned.

She hadn't yet told James about what had happened with the bearded collie pup and the Mafia's aborted mission to Wolff County. He had enough to worry about tonight without that. Getting distracted by her goals would take his focus off Rocky.

After a couple of circuits around the room, Kinney relaxed a little. The dogs were calm and composed, and no one stared at her as if she didn't belong. In fact, the only one paying any attention to her at all was Madison Parker, who was trying to hold up her camera and her black dress at the same time. Someone needed to tape that girl in properly.

James decided to give Rocky a recess outside and Kinney took the opportunity to move closer to the mayor. The throngs thinned suddenly as the hors d'oeuvres came out. When push came to shove—and it did at the buffet table—people preferred free food to political power.

Finally, she was face to face with Mayor Bradshaw, resplendent in his tuxedo. He treated her to one of his movie star smiles and held out his hand. Lately he'd complained publicly about the endless bone-crushing handshakes of his professional life, and tonight he offered only the tips of his fingers. Kinney took them and wondered if she was supposed to curtsey and deliver a kiss.

"Hello, my dear, you look lovely this evening," he said.

"Thank you, sir. I appreciate your recognition of the

charity I've backed for years. We've helped hundreds of kids in Dorset Hills get access to sport and recreation."

His smile expanded, reminding her of the wolf in Little Red Riding Hood. Well, she was no gullible lass. This man would take her down mercilessly if he had the chance. At least as soon as he realized who she was. Unless she was much mistaken, the hair and dress had thoroughly fooled him. Evie had been right.

"That's a lovely dog you have," he said. "Is it a Belgian shepherd?"

She nodded. "I'm surprised you know that, sir. Few people can tell the difference from a German shepherd."

"I've been getting thoroughly briefed on different breeds," he said, sighing. "There are so many."

"Close to 400 from what I've heard. Why trouble yourself with all those details, sir? You must have more pressing concerns as leader of this city."

"So true. It's a full-time job just to stay centered and mindful. But my staff convinced me I should know about all the breeds for a special pro—" His eyes widened and he caught himself. "Just to be able to relate to people better. Every day there's a new breed in town, it seems."

"It's wonderful, isn't it?" Kinney said. "I'd be happy to offer my help with your special dog breed project."

He shook his head quickly. "I've said too much. I want it to be a grand surprise but it will take some time, I'm afraid."

"I understand, sir," Kinney said. Whiskey pressed into her leg, as if he knew she needed the encouragement to make her pitch. She touched his ears gently for luck. "Since I have this rare moment with you, do you mind if I ask a question?"

Sipping his champagne, the mayor's smile returned. He was on familiar ground now. People were always asking for things and he was used to fielding their requests. "How can I help you, Miss...?"

"Sir, I believe I can help *you*," she said, sidestepping the re-introduction. "I recently had the chance to meet Clarence Dayton and he's very eager to speak with you about using his family estate to the fullest."

The mayor's smile switched off suddenly. "We've found Mr. Dayton very difficult in the past."

Kinney kept her fingers on Whiskey's head, hoping to draw strength from him without unsettling him with her nerves. "Clarence admits that himself, sir. But he was so impressed with the Easter festival that he decided he wants to support the City. I believe he has some exciting opportunities in mind."

"So the old man's had a change of heart?" Mayor Bradshaw said. "I guess that happens in our twilight years. Well, I'd like to hear what Clarence has to say. I'll tell my staff to set up some time with you, Miss...?"

This time she couldn't sidestep. "Butterfield. Kinney Butterfield."

His eyes narrowed and he stared at her more closely. "I know that name. You're not part of that radical rescue group, are you?"

"I used to work for the CCD," she said. "But I've been volunteering as a mediator in my spare time. In my previous employment, I saw how many contentious situations could be avoided or resolved with a simple conversation where both people felt seen and understood."

His dark eyes settled on hers. "All that begins with trust, Miss Butterfield. How do I know you have the City's interests at heart?"

"I sincerely believe that Clarence and the City can mutually benefit from this discussion, sir." She offered her own fingertips. "I'm sure your people know where to find me."

Turning, she walked as briskly to an alcove as her heels allowed and pressed her back against the cool marble wall. Breathing deeply, she said, "Whiskey, thank you. You're the best wing-dog a girl could have." He panted up at her, in what looked like a smile. "We'll get you out of here before long, buddy. I bet you feel as trapped as I do."

Poking her head around the pillar, she looked for James. He saw her and came over. "How did it go with the mayor?"

"Pretty well, I think. At least until he realized who I was. I won't be able to pull off the Cinderella disguise again."

Laughing, he handed her Rocky's leash. "I need to visit the boys' room. Do you mind?"

"Got it covered," she said. "Rocky's such a gentleman now."

When James left, she peered around the pillar again, just in time to see a dark-haired man pulling the mayor aside. They slipped into another alcove for a private discussion.

"I'd know that hair anywhere," she muttered. "It belongs on a Ken doll. Come on, boys. Let's see if we can hear what they're saying."

Walking on tiptoe with the two dogs following, she crept over to the mayor's alcove.

"I told you, I don't want any trouble," the mayor said. "Make this go away, Cobb. We can revisit the project when those pests find another big cause. In fact, *give* them one. They're always up for a new fight."

"But sir, we can't just leave those puppies to—"

"Come back when you have solutions. And keep in mind that I cannot handle more stress right now."

"We should—"

Whatever Wyatt said was cut off by a tug on Kinney's arm and a woman's sharp scream.

Rocky tried to back up between Kinney's legs and when her dress blocked him, he pushed her along a few feet, away from the mayor's alcove. She flailed to keep her balance on dangerous heels and nearly went down. It would have been funny under different circumstances.

Meanwhile an older woman advanced on her. "All I tried to do was hug that gorgeous dog and he growled," she said.

"He did not growl," Kinney said. "He's been pressed against me the whole time so I would have known. Anyway, it's not a good idea to hug any dog you don't know, ma'am."

The woman stood up to her full height on sensible flats. "Well, it's not a good idea to have a dog you can't hug at a public gathering in Dorset Hills."

Kinney stared down at her. "Is this a setup?"

"Pardon me?" The woman's grey curls shook in indignation, but her eyes darted around nervously until they landed on Madison Parker. No doubt she'd caught the interaction.

"No one goes around hugging large breeds. Who told you to do this? Or better yet, *paid* you to do this?"

The woman flushed an ugly puce and backed away. "You'll be sorry."

There was a rush of footsteps and James arrived. "Is she complaining about Rocky?"

Kinney nodded. "I think it was a setup to test us."

His blue eyes blazed. "Kinney, all I asked you to do was hold him for a few minutes. Now he's in trouble again."

She felt the color drain from her face. "I'm sorry, James. I got distracted for a second, that's all. I'm sure it will be fine."

"I'm glad you have such confidence in this town's mercy." He turned to walk away with Rocky marching by his side. "I certainly don't."

CHAPTER TWENTY-ONE

Cori was sitting on a desk at the front of the room swinging her legs when Kinney walked into the church basement. She'd come early to get a chance to chat privately before everyone else arrived.

"Welcome to the last class of your Miracle Makeover," she said, grinning. "Are you feeling like a new woman? With a new dog?"

Kinney somehow managed to nod, shake her head and shrug at the same time. "I'm not sure it's enough. Whiskey was amazing at the mayor's reception last night, but I have no idea how he'll do during the exam. The time's passed so fast."

"You've worked hard," Cori said, tossing out a bit of praise like a liver treat. "You should be fine."

"Even you're not sure." Kinney stared down at Whiskey and found he was already looking at her.

"I see good eye contact, which didn't exist a month ago. This dog wants to please you, and you're showing solid leadership most of the time. It's a far cry from how you handled Kali."

Kinney nodded. "I realize now just how much I let Kali

down." Her heart contracted as she thought about her beloved golden retriever. How she wished for a do-over, but cancer gave them no second chance.

"Now you know better and you do better," Cori said. "But you still get distracted, and if you're distracted, Whiskey's distracted."

She stared at Cori, wondering if she knew. "I won't be distracted on the fourth."

Cori shrugged. "You didn't think you'd be distracted last night either, did you? Only it was Rocky who paid the price."

Okay, so she knew. What didn't Cori know? It was like she had two-way glass into every room in the city.

"I had a good reason for being distracted. Mayor Bradshaw was talking to Wyatt Cobb about the missing puppies. Wyatt was about to propose a plan when that woman tried to hug Rocky. I think it was a set up—maybe by Madison Parker, since she was in the right place at the right time."

"The mayor's office probably wanted you out of the running before the fourth. Whiskey may have been the real target." She hopped off the table and stretched like a cat. "Look, I understand why you shifted your focus to the mayor, and in a way, I'm glad you did. But it still leaves the fact that you weren't attuned to the dogs and that's how trouble happens."

Kinney hung her head and stared at the dirty tile floor. "I know, and I feel sick about it. James must hate me."

"Well, if I'm honest, your canoodling is a distraction from the task at hand, too," Cori said.

"Who even says 'canoodling'?" Kinney glared at her. "If anything, our—our *friendship*—has helped the dogs. But I wasn't a very good friend to him and Rocky last night."

"The problem with rescue work," Cori said, still stretching out her athletic limbs, "is that it doesn't mix with much else. Last night you put the needs of the many ahead of the few. It happens. But there are always consequences." For once her expression was compassionate. "That's why I stay single. I can only juggle so many—"

"Never mind, I get it. It wouldn't have been so bad if I'd explained to James why I was following the mayor. I just didn't want him to know the City's setting a trap for us. He'd worry."

"See? No strings is the way to go," Cori said. "I may not canoodle, but my dog behaves perfectly and I can devote myself to the Mafia two hundred per cent."

Kinney sighed. "Others have both. Bridget does."

"Sullivan doesn't know the half of what we get up to," Cori said. "I'm not a good liar, in case you haven't noticed."

"I did notice, actually," Kinney said, cracking a smile. "It's the killer whale in the room."

"Killer whale?" Cori started to distribute toys and equipment. "I'd prefer a nice little shark."

"Be kind for a second and tell me if you think I'll pass this test, Cori. I can't even imagine losing Whiskey now."

Cori tossed a squeaky toy and watched as Kinney let it hit her and fall to the floor. "Good. You stayed focus. Keep that up and you should be okay."

"Should. Always with the qualifiers."

"I don't have a crystal ball, and animals can be unpredictable. On top of that, the mayor's team is unpredictable. Who knows what games they might play? All I can tell you is that you've done your work as well as you can in a short time. Your best strategy is to relax, trust the dog and trust yourself."

Kinney drew in a long shaky breath. "Okay."

Cori gave a little smirk. "And trust me to help if something does go wrong. If they mess with my Miracle Makeover dogs, there will be hell to pay."

That gave Kinney more comfort than she expected. It was good to know Cori had her back.

Whiskey turned quickly and she knew James had come into the room. Part of her worried he wouldn't show tonight, simply to avoid her. But Rocky's needs outweighed his annoyance. There was no question he was still mad. James had a genial expression by nature but his eyes had become glacial. Instead of joining her at the front of the room, he stayed near the door.

When class began, Cori went through a few last drills before sending everyone off. "Pick a neighborhood that you know will be full of distractions and expose your dogs to their triggers," she said. "Call me if you need anything. Otherwise, we'll meet again on the fourth. Party to follow at Runaway Farm."

James went out to the parking lot and she hurried after him. "Are you leaving without me?"

"I figure I can give Rocky my full attention without distractions," he said.

"James, come on. Let's do our last assignment together. I can explain what happened on the way. But you must know I want Rocky to succeed. It would break my heart if either of our dogs failed that test. Let's work them hard tonight."

After a second, he nodded. "Riverdale?"

"Riverdale it is," she said. "If you don't mind, I think walking Whiskey on his old street would be a good way to make sure he's rock steady."

During the short drive, she filled him in about the bearded collie puppy and the Mafia stakeout. "I think they're setting a trap for us, so we walked away," she said. "But now we know they're decoying purebred puppies from Animal Services and dumping them somewhere. It may be at that site in Wolff County, or that could be a red herring."

James shook his head as he parked on a side street near Whiskey's former home with the Barber family. "I don't like that they're deliberately luring you into a snare," he said. "If you guys got up to your usual tricks, they could arrest you."

"I know. That's why we stepped back. Meanwhile we know that they're gathering puppies for some special project, and who knows how well they're being treated?"

"How do you know about this special project?" he asked, getting out of the car.

She got out too and spoke to him across the hood. "Because I was eavesdropping on the mayor and Wyatt Cobb, the dog cop, while you were in the men's room last night. That's why I wasn't paying enough attention to Rocky." She held up her hand. "I know it doesn't justify it, but I wasn't just being frivolous. And I'm so sorry, James."

His icy eyes thawed slightly and he leaned on the car for a few seconds before speaking again. "Okay. I think we'd better get to the bottom of this puppy project before the Fourth of July. Otherwise, how can you give Whiskey your full attention?"

"Before the fourth? That's only two days."

"Miracles happen in two days. You'll see. For now, we've got an assignment."

Kinney was dying to hear what James had in mind, but she wanted to prove she could put the dogs first. She owed him that. So she kept quiet while they walked down one street, around the corner, and past the house where Whiskey spent six traumatic weeks. She was careful to relax her shoulders and arms, clear her mind and breathe evenly, so that the energy she fed through the leash was positive.

The dog knew exactly where he was, no doubt about that. As they got closer to the house, his ears came forward, his tail rose and he made a soft snorting sound as he took it all in. No matter how tempted he was, however, he stayed in position and the leash didn't even tighten. Once they'd passed the Barbers' front walk, his tail dropped. Then it sank even further, curling right under him, as they passed Myrtle McCabe's home. Kinney moved forward briskly and confidently, and his tail lifted again with every step.

"Well done," James said, smiling at Kinney.

"Such a good boy," she said. "I'd fall all over him right now if I didn't think Cori had eyes on us."

"Let's head down the street to that crowd," James said, pointing. "That'll be a good test for Rocky."

Whiskey's muzzle went up and he sniffed. Then he started pulling towards the crowd. "What is it, boy?" she asked. She didn't try to stop him; he never did this unless he had a good reason.

Nearly 20 people had gathered in front of the remains of a large home that was in the midst of renovation. It had been gutted to the foundation and there was scaffolding and boarding surrounding it. A high metal fence surrounded the property but it was bent back in one corner. Whiskey pulled her to the open corner and whined.

Kinney turned to the closest person and asked, "What's going on?"

"Myrtle McCabe's wolfhound got loose and ran in there after a rabbit," the woman said. "Someone's gone to get Myrtle. The dog's deaf so it's not responding to us."

Kinney turned to James. "Do you mind if I help?"

He rolled his eyes. "As if I could stop you."

She handed Whiskey's leash to him. "He's terrified of Myrtle. Please don't be as cavalier as I was with your dog."

"Go," he said, smiling. "Be the dog cop."

Whiskey struggled to follow, but she told him sternly, "Stay."

Slipping through the gap in the fence, she walked carefully over the rubble to squeeze behind the boarding. "Heidi," she called. The dog might not hear its name but she knew it felt vibrations. She wasn't expecting a high-pitched human voice to call back. "Help! I'm stuck."

Kinney poked her head back around the boards and yelled, "There's a kid stuck back here. Someone call 911."

The woman she'd spoken to before covered her mouth in horror. "I saw Liam Barber poking around here. I bet he went after the dog."

Kinney's stomach took a perilous dip. "Liam?" she called, going back in. "Liam? It's Kinney. Remember me? Whiskey's new owner?"

"Kinney!" The voice was faint and far away. "We fell into the hole. Help!"

"Coming, buddy! Hang tight!"

There was still plenty of light to watch her step as she crossed the boards workers had set up as a walkway. She looked around for tools, and found a long pole with a hook on the end. That could help, but rope would be better. There was a mid-sized bin made of wood with a lock on it that looked promising. Swinging the pole hard, she bashed through one of the slats. Then it was easy enough to pry open. Inside she found an assortment of tools, a flashlight, and to her relief, a long stretch of yellow nylon rope.

"Kinney!" Liam called. "Where are you?"

"Coming. Are you hurt?"

"No. But Heidi's limping."

She shone the light into the basement excavation. Liam's pale face looked up at her while the big wolfhound crouched by his side. "Hang on," she said. "We'll bring Heidi up first."

She threaded the rope through a hole in the rim of a large metal dumpster and tied it off securely. Then she tossed the rope down to Liam. "Do you think you can wrap this around Heidi and tie her up tight? I can tell you how to make the knots, okay?"

Liam followed her instructions to a tee. Then she got up and found some long, heavy boards and dragged them over to the side of the new basement.

"Lead the dog over to the other side," she said, shining the light down. "Be really careful and cover your head. I'm going to make a ramp."

She lowered the first board and maneuvered it into position. The second proved more unwieldy. The third seemed to come alive under her hands and refused to comply. She was running out of strength. There was no way the dog would walk up such a narrow ramp.

Suddenly big hands joined hers on the board. "I got this."

She looked up at James gratefully. "Where are the dogs?"

"In the car. Myrtle came down the road screaming like a banshee and it wasn't fair to either dog. So I got a few guys to restrain her and ran them back to the car."

Together, they got the ramp into position. Then James skipped down without a moment's hesitation and literally pushed the wolfhound up from behind. Liam was roped off, but he climbed the ramp like a monkey before Kinney could even get the dog untied. He threw his arms around her and she fell over on her back, with bits of concrete jabbing between her shoulder blades.

Sitting up, she hugged him. "You're amazingly brave. But you gotta be more careful, buddy. That's what dog cops are for."

"I wanna be a dog cop just like you when I grow up."

She laughed. "That's not really my job anymore, but it's always good to look out for animals."

"How's Whiskey?" Liam asked. His eyes shone with

tears and Kinney hugged him again. "He's doing great. I'm so lucky you let me have him that day."

"Mom said it was for the best," Liam said, swallowing hard. "Aunt Jacinda, too. But I hope my dad will let me have a dog one day."

"I bet he will," she said, her heart easing at his words. "Especially after he hears what a hero you were tonight."

James cleared his throat to remind them to get moving. He led the way out, with the dog behind him and Kinney holding Liam's hand. The sirens were just coming up the street, but their screaming couldn't equal Myrtle McCabe's. Liam's mom was busting a lung herself and both women fell to their knees to hug their lost kids.

Myrtle was the first to rise and she opened her arms to Kinney. Stepping back, Kinney held up her hands. "Don't. You can thank us by being kinder to animals in the future." She lowered her voice. "Because of your abuse, however, I have the best dog in the world. So we'll leave it at that."

Myrtle shrank back and somehow her mauve hair seemed to dim. She skulked off up the street with her limping wolfhound.

Others gathered to congratulate them but James took Kinney's hand and pulled her away. "We have our own dogs to worry about," he said. "Good night, everyone."

"Never a dull moment, is there?" she asked, before pulling a splinter out of her hand with her teeth.

"People were filming that," James said as they walked hand in hand back to the car.

"It's inevitable these days. You have to run away to a hill in Wolff County to get a moment's privacy."

"If that's a hint, I'm taking it," he said, laughing as he opened the car door. "Finally, I've got a rescue war story. Do you think Cori will let me into the Mafia?"

CHAPTER TWENTY-TWO

Two hours after sunset the next evening, Kinney held the night vision goggles to her eyes with her right hand and gripped James' hand with her left. "I wish I could be down there," she said. "This feels like cheating. We Mafia take care of our own problems."

"I know," he said. "But that was when the problems were smaller and localized. Now the mayor's secrets are spreading like a fungus even beyond county lines. Sometimes you need to make the efficient decision."

"The others are going to be mad," she said. "Cori, especially."

"They'll only be mad they didn't get to see it happen," he said. "Once it's all over they'll thank you."

"Thank *me*? This is all because of you. I could never have pulled it off."

James had hired a security firm from New York to simultaneously raid all six of the potential kennel sites Kinney had been able to identify with her hacking. They didn't know which ones were in use, so it made sense to hit them all. The strategy meant that by the time City officers got their act together it would all be over.

Kinney and James sat on the hill above the site in Wolff County, because it seemed the most likely to be in use. Choosing a site outside Dorset Hills County lines gave more political wiggle room.

It was like watching a SWAT team on TV. People in black clothing and masks jumped out of vans and circled the building as if choreographed. There was a loud pop and glass tinkling, and most of the security people disappeared, except for three on watch.

The next few minutes stretched out and James whispered, "Breathe."

"You don't have to whisper," she said. "We're alone."

They both laughed a bit and then held their breath again.

"Oh my gosh!" Kinney said. A man came out of the building holding a squirming dog under each arm. Others did the same, and they made a human chain to pass all the pups into one of the vans. Even from their vantage point above, they could hear barking and whining.

"Hurry, hurry," Kinney whispered.

It was already over. Everyone jumped back into the vans and drove off. They kept their lights off but they didn't rush. It ended up looking like a state funeral.

James turned the SUV around, and when the vans passed, the last one flashed its lights. He pulled in behind it, and followed.

Kinney was already texting the others. "911. Runaway Farm. Stat."

Long before they reached the farm, two of the three vans veered off. Only the one holding the puppies continued on. James moved ahead and led it down under the tall arch and down the winding driveway. Glancing in his rearview mirror, he said, "There's another van. One of the other sites must have been active."

Cori, Bridget, Duff, Maisie and Nika were already at the farm with Hannah when they arrived, and Evie and Remi pulled up soon after. Ari careened down the drive like the devil was after her. Flynn, Mim and Sasha came last.

James guided the vans to back up to the barn and once again a human chain unloaded the dogs and puppies, and set them in the two empty pens in the barn. There were 26 in all, and they appeared to be purebreds all under a year old. Bridget leaned into the pen and picked up the little bearded collie and cuddled it. Her blingy collar was gone now.

Outside, James spoke to the men in black and then waved the vans off.

Cori was inside one of the pens, inspecting each dog in turn. "They seem to be fine," she said. "We need to divide them up and get them to foster families tonight—as far out of Dog Town as possible."

She worked with Bridget to make the calls, and one by one, people drove off with their canine cargo. When nearly everyone had gone, Cori and Bridget turned to Kinney. "Was it only the two sites?"

Kinney nodded. "The rest were empty or incomplete. That doesn't mean there aren't others."

Cori stared from Kinney to James and back. Kinney waited for an explosion that didn't come. "As much as I hate to admit it, we couldn't have pulled that off," she said, at last. "I know our limits."

"She's thanking you," Kinney told James. "You don't know how shocking that is."

Cori flipped a couple of orange flashes at Kinney and let out a long breath. "Whew. That feels better. Being nice... it costs me."

Kinney laughed and went to grab two dog carriers from the barn. "I'll deliver these little guys," she said.

Taking the carriers from her, Cori shook her head. "You two are off duty. You need to get your beauty rest before the exam tomorrow." Loading the pups in the back seat of her truck, she called back, "Alone, you hear? No canoodling before a big competition."

Bridget shrugged, and got into the van with two other pups.

Kinney watched them go, holding hands with James. "That was a huge win," she said. "But tomorrow's loss would feel even bigger."

"We won't lose," he said, walking her to the Prius. Looking up at the vast sky dotted with stars, he added, "We're the good guys. Someone's gotta be looking out for us."

RED VELVET ROPE cordoned off a big ring in Bellington Square, in front of the bronze German shepherd. There were five stations set up inside the circle, as well as a low platform for the final ruling. The dogs from the Miracle Makeover Program needed to move through the stations one by one. Each offered a specific challenge designed to test for canine flaws.

Mayor Bradshaw and some of his sycophants sat in a fancy box specially designed for the event, that stood about six feet over the proceedings.

He waved a baton to tell the master of ceremonies to begin the test. Jenny Kent went first with Angus the Scottie. The dog had been the most stubborn of any in the program but Jenny had worked tirelessly with him and it showed today. He trotted calmly by her side and jumped on a small stage for the first challenge, which was performing basic commands without treats or other incentives. Sit. Stand. Down. Stay. Leave it. Drop it. Jenny circled the platform and the Scottie's rectangular head swivelled to watch her. At the next station, he had to approach and meet several strangers, all of whom leaned down to pat him. The third challenge was Angus's weak spot: he had to walk right through a small pen containing live, squawking chickens. As a dog with a high prey drive, it was probably torture, but he made it with only one slight leash correction from Jenny. The fourth station required walking through an enclosure of shrieking children banging and clanging musical instruments. The fifth was a pen of energetic dogs, all off leash, which was managed by Cori herself. Sixth, and last, they stepped onto the long platform to wait. The final test would occur when all the dogs were ready and in position.

Brianne went next with Nugget and passed without a single error. The two young men with their bull terrier crosses also did well, with only a couple of minor blips in the pen full of dogs.

The master of ceremonies tapped James and Rocky to go next. Kinney was last on the list, presumably as the poster girl for the program.

She held her breath as James and Rocky set off. The big dog moved with his usual deliberation, but today he kept pace with James and even looked up at him occasionally for direction. James walked with calm authority and he no longer pleaded with Rocky to do his bidding. She couldn't even hear his quiet commands. He preferred to use hand gestures instead of saying anything at all.

The first challenge went well, and they went on to meet the strangers. Rocky bounced for a second on his paws but simmered down with one look from James. Six different people patted Rocky one by one on different parts of his body. The dog was stoic, like the statue that loomed over them. After succeeding at that, the rest went smoothly. Rocky ignored the clanging children and the chickens completely. The pen of dogs brought his ruff up momentarily, but a look from Cori settled it so fast the judges may not have noticed. When they reached the platform at the end, Kinney raised her hand in a salute and James returned it, grinning.

Finally, it was her turn. Squatting, she spoke to Whiskey. "This is it, buddy. They're going to try to spook you, but I've got your back. Whatever happens, it's you and me. Got that?"

He leaned over and licked her face and an "awww" rippled through the crowd.

The master of ceremonies clapped and called for silence.

Whiskey whizzed through his basic commands and happily submitted to being greeted by strangers. He was very much interested in herding the chickens, but Kinney urged him on. The next station with the children banging on instruments was going to be a tough one. His big ears went down and his tail followed suit. But Kinney spoke in a quiet, confident voice to assure him that tuneless music offered no threat. The pen of dogs brought his tail and ears back up and he wagged enthusiastically. He tried a play pose, but Kinney kept him moving forward to the platform.

She exchanged wary glances with James. That had all seemed a bit too easy. Surely there was a grenade waiting to go off? Perhaps literally, to frighten her dog to death.

After taking her assigned position at the end of the row, Kinney felt Whiskey turn. Then he let out a long, low whine that sounded like pain and joy combined. Following his glance, she saw something that made her stomach flip and plunge. It was Jacinda Allen and her husband, Whiskey's original owners. Last Kinney had heard, Jacinda was overseas on tour. Now she was right here, ringside. Was she hoping to reclaim the dog who adored her? The dog Kinney now adored more than she'd thought possible?

He started to pull on his leash and she hissed for him to stop. She tried to catch Jacinda's eye but the woman had locked onto Whiskey like a sniper. "Hey, Whiskey," she called.

That was it.

The dog dashed off the riser, ripping the leash from Kinney's hand, and raced to his former owner. She knelt and took him into her arms, laughing and crying. He let out a drawn-out wail that brought tears to every eye on the platform, including James'. Kinney took one look at him and broke down.

Whiskey had chosen Jacinda.

Jacinda had been gone for months, whereas Kinney had made this dog the center of her universe, working and playing hard with him day and night. Yet Whiskey still loved Jacinda more. He had never made those sounds for Kinney, and every whimper broke her heart all over. After all her struggles, she wasn't enough for this dog.

James threw his arm around her and whispered, "It's not about you. She just came first, that's all. Dogs don't know any better."

Kinney sat down on the edge of the platform, worried she might actually faint. Hundreds of people were staring at her, and Madison's camera zoomed in to catch every tear.

Cori got out of the dog pen and ran over to her. "Don't you fall apart on me, Kinney Butterfield."

Tears streamed down Kinney's face. "It's like losing Kali all over." She realized that when her guard was down, Whiskey had surreptitiously taught her to love again. That, in turn, left her wide open to the terrible pain of loss. "I can't, Cori. I can't."

"You can. This is what comes of loving dogs, Kinney. The joy and the pain go hand in hand." Cori's dark eyes filled, too—something Kinney couldn't remember seeing before. "You need to pick up and go on." She reached out and shook Kinney's arm gently. "That's what we all do. Because not loving them is not living."

Wiping her face with her bare arm, Kinney shook her head. "No."

Cori shook her arm harder. "Yes. Get up and call Whiskey. He will come."

Kinney sobbed harder. "I won't. He deserves to be happy. If he wants her, I stand down."

"This isn't a love test," Cori said. "That woman can't provide the stable home he needs right now, and the dog knows it, trust me."

It *was* a love test, though. Kinney had seen how bonded Whiskey was to Jacinda back in January. It wasn't fair to expect him to switch allegiances when that option opened again. She had always been second best to this dog.

There was a rush of air and she felt the impact of fur hitting her bent head. Whiskey was leaping around, trying to lick her face. She raised her head and he stared at her with bright eyes. It was like he was saying, "Break's over. Let's get back to work."

Cori gave Kinney a shove. "Get up and take your position. If you pass this test, it'll be a freaking miracle."

The participants stood in a line, with dogs seated at their sides. From above, the mayor yelled, "Fire!"

Kinney wasn't sure how many pistols shot off at once, but every dog in sight reacted, including the cavorting pups in the pen Cori had left. Some barked, some whined, many dropped to the ground shaking. But all of the dogs on the platform stood firm.

There was a long, still pause afterwards, during which Kinney's ears rang. It was like everything happened in slow motion. She looked down and locked eyes with Whiskey. He didn't so much as flinch. He had passed this challenge—his worst—with aplomb. It meant she had successfully rehabilitated him from his trauma, and for that she was grateful, even if he went home today with Jacinda.

The Master of Ceremonies called for attention and announced the verdicts. One by one, each person stepped forward with their dog and got a red ribbon signifying they'd passed the test. Jenny and Brianne were crying now, too. James and Rocky were both impassive as they received their red ribbon, and James turned anxiously to Kinney.

After a dramatic pause, the MC declared: "I regret to say that Ms. Kinney Butterfield and Whiskey have failed the exam. The dog disobeyed and broke away, which could have resulted in injury. Officer Wyatt Cobb will speak with Miss Butterfield now about the implications."

Wyatt stepped forward in his CCD uniform, looking as uncomfortable as his plastic Ken doll face allowed. Whatever he'd been ordered to say to Kinney didn't sit easily.

Before he got a chance to say it, a sensible shoe came out of the crowd and kicked Wyatt hard enough to send him reeling backwards.

The foot was attached to Myrtle McCabe, who shoved past Wyatt and then wrestled the mic from the MC. "I will not stand by in silence while the City makes another stupid decision," she said, aiming another sharp kick at a security guard. "Kinney Butterfield saved my dog the other night. She's saved two others that I know about and likely far more." She shook her fist at the mayor's box. "What are you thinking, Bill? And what has this stupid town become if you fail someone like Kinney Butterfield at anything at all? She should be celebrated, not sanctioned." Raising her arm, she shouted, "Boo, Billy Bradshaw. Boo!"

As the crowd picked up the "Boo, Billy" and ran with it, Mayor Bradshaw rose, swept out of the booth and hustled into City Hall with his followers. The MC managed to seize the mic and quickly backtracked, declaring all dogs winners, including Whiskey. Security guards began dispersing the crowd to enjoy the various activities throughout the town's center.

Jacinda slipped under the velvet rope and came toward Kinney. It was the moment of truth.

"I'm so sorry for creating such a distraction," she said, kneeling to embrace Whiskey again. "And after you were so good to us last winter. The City offered to fly me home for the event and insisted I stand where I did." Her eyes filled as she looked up. "I wasn't sure Whiskey would even remember me. My sister told me you'd adopted him and were taking such good care of him. I don't know how I can ever thank you enough. He's an amazing dog."

"That he is," Kinney said. "I love this dog. But if you're here to take him back, I understand. You made him what he is."

She shook her head. "I made him a good dog. You made him a great dog."

"Excuse me," Cori said, joining them. "Most of the credit goes to me for the greatness. I've got this failproof Miracle Makeover Program, you see."

Everyone laughed and it lightened the mood. "Anyway," Jacinda continued, "I wouldn't think of breaking you up. But even if I'd wanted to, Whiskey's made his own decision."

While Kinney was distracted, the dog had wedged

himself firmly between Kinney's feet and was trying to worm his big body backwards. Her legs had bowed into a most unflattering pose. She looked at James, and he turned away, snickering.

Moving aside, Kinney hugged Jacinda in a formal handoff and invited her and her husband to attend the after-party at Runaway Farm. Once they'd disappeared into the crowd, Kinney dropped to her knees and hugged Whiskey, burying her face in his fur and murmuring, "All mine."

James offered his hand and when she stood, he leaned in and whispered, "See? He chose you after all. Who wouldn't?"

Kinney looked up at him and drew a deep breath. Just months ago, her heart had felt like a hard, cold fist that would never unclench. Now, it turned out that there was room in it for two new loves.

Cori rolled her eyes in disgust. "Would you two just go to the farm and get a stall?"

CHAPTER TWENTY-THREE

Hannah Pemberton knew how to throw a party. Since the dramatic raid and rescue the night before, Runaway Farm had been completely made over in Fourth of July mode. There were red, white and blue streamers everywhere, cute little fast food booths, and games of chance to rival the midway at a county fair. People had gravitated there long before the City's formal celebrations ended, just because it was becoming a destination of choice.

"I take full credit for the crowd," Evie said, panning around with her video camera. "The Princess and the Pig continues to pull them in."

"How come you get the credit and I get the embarrassment and the bills?" Hannah asked, smiling.

"It's tough to be a star, isn't it?" Evie asked. "Mayor Bradshaw is going to be even more annoyed that people are spurning his party for yours."

"Well, I do have a secret weapon," Hannah said.

That weapon was Alvina, possibly the most popular alpaca on the planet. Someone had brought out a boombox and people were lining up to dance with her. Remi had set out a collection jar for charity, but reminded everyone that you can't force an alpaca to dance when the mood's passed. Somehow, the mood didn't pass. She kept on going until Charlie came to put her in the barn for a rest. She thanked him by spitting in his face, and Evie was there to catch it all for posterity.

Kinney and James walked hand in hand through the crowd with the dogs, feeling almost like celebrities themselves. Every time someone mentioned the big moment where Whiskey made his choice, however, Kinney would cry. She gave up trying to salvage her mascara.

"I'm not that big on makeup anyway," James said, as she dabbed her eyes. "It doesn't quite jive with a thrill seeker like you."

The waterworks started all over when she saw the Barber family. Even Dan had come out, and his harsh edges seemed to have softened a little. As Evie had predicted, exposure to goats brought smiles even to those with troubled hearts. Ginny and Liam hugged Kinney, and Dan shook her hand. "I'm sorry," he said. "If Old Lady McCabe can turn things around like that, I can do better, too."

Kinney laughed through her tears. "Then do me a favor and let Liam visit Whiskey now and then. I could use a walking buddy sometimes."

After nodding agreement, Dan followed Liam as he ran gleefully to see Alvina.

Wiping the dark circles under her eyes, Kinney took James' hand. "I want to look more polished for my new consulting business. I've decided to start mediating for pet owners in conflict throughout the greater Dog Town area."

"Fantastic," he said. "Do you need to find a storefront? I can help with start-up."

She shook her head. "It's sweet of you to offer, James, but

I'm not comfortable taking your money unless it's for rescue work. Then you're welcome to be as generous as you please."

"Money can't buy our way out of everything," Cori said, coming up behind them. "It's going to take good, old-fashioned surveillance work to stay ahead of this mayor."

"She's right about that," Evie said. "James' ploy worked once and it will set the mayor back in whatever he's planning. But he'll rebound. He always does. He still has the properties and there's a plan we don't know about."

"The war begins again tomorrow," Cori said, as all the rest of the Mafia—and their partners—joined them. An event like this brought all the men out, too.

"At least we freed all the puppies," Kinney said. "That's something."

Arianna Torrance pushed through the crowd like she meant business. "I've just had a terrible shock," she said. "After delivering those two rescue pups to Brenton last night, I stayed over with my parents. When I was driving back today, I stopped to visit a client. Imagine my shock to find their gorgeous 10-month-old doodle—one of my finest—is gone."

"Gone where?" Kinney asked.

Ari's already flushed face turned scarlet. "They sold her a month ago. To someone who offered three times what they paid for her."

"Why are you just hearing about it? Isn't that sort of thing in your contract?"

"You bet it is. They thought they could get away with it. That I'd never find out. Now they're on a list with another breeder to replace her on the cheap."

"That's terrible," Kinney said. "It sounds like what happened with the couple I mentioned." She pointed to Trina and Joey, who were managing to keep their Rhodesian ridgeback more or less under control, after some private sessions with Cori.

Ari looked around and lowered her voice. "I think I'm being targeted. When I started randomly calling clients, two others admitted they'd recently sold their dogs. No one has much information on the buyer. It was a cash transfer and a dead drop." Her blue eyes filled. "I can't believe people would just sell my babies, especially after waiting so long for them. Who knows where they are?"

"We'll get to the bottom of this," Bridget said, patting her shoulder. "I'm starting to agree with Evie that we need to get this mayor ousted. And I think I know how to get the ball rolling."

"How?" a dozen voices chimed at once.

Bridget signaled them to huddle. "If Dorset Hills is going this far off the rails, it's time we called on the person who basically created this mess to come back and fix it."

"Isla McInnis?" Cori said, frowning. "She'll never come. She's some sort of corporate bigwig now and wants nothing to do with us."

"We can get her back," Bridget said. "I'm sure of it."

Flynn Strathmore had been leaning against the fence of Alvina's pen, quietly sketching through the entire conversation. She passed the sketchbook to Bridget. The illustration featured a beautiful dark-haired woman with a fierce dog standing in Bellington Square. The dog looked like a boxer, and wore a tag that read "Hera." In her other hand, the woman held a bridal bouquet.

"That's her! Ilsa McInnis," Bridget said. "Only she owns a terrier mix."

Flynn shrugged. "That's what I see. Send it to her and see what happens."

Bridget nodded. "What do we have to lose?"

"We have everything to lose," Kinney said. "But we're certainly going to fight this mayor to the bitter end."

The entire group gave a cheer.

"That's a plan for tomorrow," Hannah said. "Today we celebrate smaller victories. I believe Alvina's had enough rest. Who's up next?"

James offered his hand to Kinney. "May Alvina and I have the honor?"

Kinney gave Whiskey's leash to Cori and practically skipped over to the gate. "Dorset Hills may be going insane," she said, "but at least we have things like this to keep us grounded."

"You call dancing with an alpaca sane?" James said, grinning as Alvina gave him a deep bow.

"It's about as sane as I want to be," Kinney said, as they both returned her bow.

"Enough talk," James said, hopping on the spot and pumping his arms. "Show us you've got moves."

She did a quick pirouette, struck a pose and then took off with James and the alpaca in pursuit. The sound of the crowd faded quickly, even the barking. In that moment, there was just love, laughter and thundering hooves.

Are you ready for the thrilling conclusion to this year-in-the-life of Dog Town? If so, get your paws on *Better or Worse in Dog Town*. I promise it will not disappoint!

Please sign up for my author newsletter at **Sandyrideout.com** to receive the FREE prequel, *Ready* *or Not in Dog Town,* as well as *A Dog with Two Tales,* the prequel to the Bought-the-Farm series. You'll also get the latest news and far too many pet photos.

Before you move on to the next book, if you would be so kind as to leave a review of this one, that would be great. I appreciate the feedback and support. Reviews stoke the fires of my creativity!

Other Books by Sandy Rideout and Ellen Riggs

Dog Town Series:

- *Ready or Not in Dog Town* (The Beginning)
- *Bitter and Sweet in Dog Town* (Labor Day)
- *A Match Made in Dog Town* (Thanksgiving)
- *Lost and Found in Dog Town* (Christmas)
- *Calm and Bright in Dog Town* (Christmas)
- *Tried and True in Dog Town* (New Year's)
- *Yours and Mine in Dog Town* (Valentine's Day)
- *Nine Lives in Dog Town* (Easter)
- *Great and Small in Dog Town* (Memorial Day)
- *Bold and Blue in Dog Town* (Independence Day)
- *Better or Worse in Dog Town* (Labor Day)

Boxed Sets:

- *Mischief in Dog Town - Books 1-3*
- *Mischief in Dog Town - Books 4-7*
- *Mischief in Dog Town - Books 8-10*

Bought-the-Farm Cozy Mystery Series

- *A Dog with Two Tales (prequel)*
- *Dogcatcher in the Rye*
- *Dark Side of the Moo*
- *A Streak of Bad Cluck*
- *Till the Cat Lady Sings*
- *Alpaca Lies*
- *Twas the Bite Before Christmas*
- *Swine and Punishment*
- *Don't Rock the Goat*
- *Swan with the Wind*